UFOs That Crashed to Earth

SR71 "Blackbird"

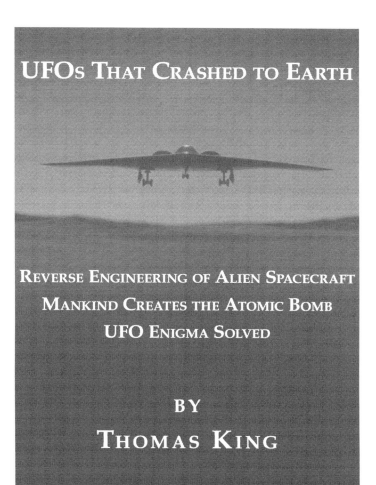

UFOs That Crashed to Earth

Reverse Engineering of Alien Spacecraft
Mankind Creates the Atomic Bomb
UFO Enigma Solved

BY
Thomas King

B2 Bomber

authorHOUSE®

AuthorHouse™
1663 Liberty Drive, Suite 200
Bloomington, IN 47403
www.authorhouse.com
Phone: 1-800-839-8640

First published by AuthorHouse 1/14/2009

ISBN: 978-1-4389-4618-4 (sc)

Printed in the United States of America
Bloomington, Indiana

This book is printed on acid-free paper.

AUTHOR'S MESSAGE
TO THE READER

"UFOs THAT CRASHED TO EARTH" IS A BOOK ABOUT MANKIND'S FUTURE AND ABOUT OUR PRESENT. FOR THE PAST SIXTY OR SEVENTY YEARS MANKIND HAS BEEN BUSY DEVELOPING AND EXPERIMENTING WITH ALL KINDS OF WEAPONS THAT COULD DESTROY OUR PLANT EARTH. NUCLEAR WEAPONS ALONE COULD WIPE US ALL OUT A HUNDRED TIMES OVER. WE ALREADY HAVE WORLD WIDE POLLUTION FROM BURNING FOSSIL FUELS AND FROM OVER 2000 NUCLEAR BOMB TESTS IN NUMEROUS COUNTRIES AROUND THE WORLD! CAN MANKIND EVER STOP HIS INSANE PURSUIT OF HIS OWN DISTRUCTION? RECENT DEVELOPMENTS IN IRAN, NORTH KOREA, PAKISTAN. INDIA AND OTHER COUNTRIES SAY NO. THESE UNSTABLE AND AGGRESSIVE PLACES NOW HAVE NUCLEAR WEAPONS AIMED AT THEIR NEIGHBORS!

THE NEW STEALTH B2 BOMBERS ARE BASED AT WHITEMAN AIR FORCE BASE NEAR THE UFO CRASH SIGHT OF 1941. CAPE GIRARDEAU, MISSOURI WAS THE CRASH SIGHT OF AN

ALIEN SPACECRAFT AND THE CRAFT AND ALIENS WERE RECOVERED. NOW, TOP SECRET B2 BOMBERS ARE BASED THERE. THE B2 CAN STRIKE THE ENEMY WITH POWERFUL NUCLEAR WEAPONS ANYWHERE IN THE WORLD AND RETURN TO BASE WITHOUT LANDING, WITH ONE IN FLIGHT RE-FUELING. THE B2 LOOKS EXACTELY LIKE THE ORIGINAL AIR FORCE "FLYING WING" OF THE 1950'S AND 60'S. THE USAF COULD NOT SOLVE CERTAIN PROBLEMS IN THE DESIGN. AFTER SEVERAL CRASHES IT WAS GROUNDED YEARS AGO AND THE PROJECT WAS FORGOTTEN UNTIL NOW. THOUGH THE B2 BOMBER OR, NEW "FLYING WING", TOOK DECADES TO PASS THE USAF'S RIDGID STANDARDS, IT IS NOW NUMBER ONE IN THE AIR FORCE'S BOMBER ARSENAL. DID AIR FORCE REVERSE ENGINEERING OF ALIEN UFO'S SOLVE THE PROBLEMS OF THE ORIGINAL FLYING WING OF THE FIFTIES AND SIXTIES?

THE FAMOUS "BLACKBIRD", SR-71, SUPERSONIC, RECON JET WAS NEVER SHOT DOWN BY ENEMY FIRE. IT WAS TESTED AT GROOM LAKE, (AREA 51) AND NELLIS AFB, NEAR AREA 51. ALTHOUGH GROUNDED NOW, AND NOT IN USE, THE BLACKBIRD STILL HOLDS THE RECORD SPEED FOR JET AIRCRAFT OF 2200 MPH AT 85,OOO FEET IN ALTITUDE. AIR FORCE AND AIRCRAFT DESIGNERS SOLVED THE PROBLEM OF METAL FOR THE OUTER SKIN BY USING A SPECIAL

TITANIAM ALOY. WHEN SEVERAL SR-71'S CRASHED THE USAF COVERED IT UP BY STATING IT WAS NOT A CRASH OF AN SR-71, BUT RATHER THAT IT WAS A CRASH OF ANOTHER JET AIRCRAFT. DID THEY WANT THE PUBLIC TO THINK IT WAS A CRASH OF AN ALIEN SPACECRAFT? AIR FORCE BRASS SAY THEY LIED TO MAINTAIN SECRECY.

THE F-117A STEALTH FIGHTER WAS TESTED AT GROOM LAKE AND AREA 51. THE AIR FORCE COVERED UP ALL CRASHES AND LIED ABOUT IT'S EXISTENCE. HOW DID ENGINEERS SOLVE THE STEALTH PROBLEM AND MAKE THE F-117A NOT APPEAR ON ENEMY RADAR? WAS IT REVERSE ENGINEERED FROM ALIEN STEALTH TECHNOLOGY? THESE LIES AND COVER UPS HAVE CREATED AN ATMOSPHERE OF DISTRUST OF THE AIR FORCE AND MILITARY BY THE PUBLIC. NOW, MOST PEOPLE BELIEVE THAT ALIEN UFO SPACECRAFT WERE RECOVERED AFTER EITHER CRASHING OR BEING SHOT DOWN AND THEN REVERSE ENGINEERED BY AERONAUTICAL ENGINEERS.

THE UFO PHENOMENON IS ONE OF THE BIGGEST MYSTERIES OF ALL TIME. ALTHOUGH THERE HAVE BEEN THOUSANDS OF SIGHTINGS OVER A PERIOD OF ALMOST ONE HUNDRED YEARS, WE ARE STILL NO CLOSER TO SOLVING THIS ENIGMA. UNIDENTIFIED FLYING OBJECTS ARE REPORTED DAILY FROM ALL OVER THE WORLD. WILL MANKIND EVER SOLVE AND UNDERSTAND THIS STRANGE

SITUATION? THE UFO SIGHTINGS AT THE TIME OF THE FIRST ATOMIC BOMB TESTS IN THE U.S. MAY HAVE BEEN A WARNING! WHY WERE THEY IGNORED?

THE CHARACTERS IN THE BOOK ATTEMPT TO SOLVE THESE PROBLEMS AND COME AWAY FROM IT WITH A RENEWED SENSE OF PURPOSE AND OUTLOOK ON LIFE. HOWEVER, THEY CANNOT SOLVE ALL OF MANKIND'S PROBLEMS.

THE ANSWERS LIE WITHIN EACH OF US.

TOM KING

TABLE OF CONTENTS

PREFACE

There have been over 2000 nuclear bombs detonated around the world. That's over two thousand! Two thousand times our Earth has been subjected to nuclear weapons and the life ending nuclear fallout! Atomic bombs, more powerful hydrogen bombs, super hydrogen "Doomsday" bombs and more and more powerful bombs are detonated over and over again. The Blue-Green planet, our lovely Earth where we all live, could be dying a slow death! Our beautiful world, the wonderful, lush and life sustaining Earth has been polluted with nuclear fallout and other forms of atomic, particle pollution over and over again for more then half a century! Our country, America has stockpiled hundreds of these nuclear weapons in storage. For our "Nuclear Weapons Arsenal", we have them on nuclear submarines, in ICBMs, in cruise missiles, on board B-52s, jet fighters, B-1 and B-2 bombers and even in artillery shells! Now they're ready to fire! Russia, Israel, England, France and many other countries have stockpiled them too. And we're not done yet! No, Mankind has some more and better, suicidal plans for all life on our planet. Plant, animal and all other life forms on Earth are in danger of being totally wiped out! North Korea, Pakistan, India, China and possibly

Iran are testing more and more of these terrible weapons. These unstable and aggressive nations are capable of almost anything, including the unthinkable!

When unused nuclear weapons are eventually disposed of it creates more nuclear waste. You may ask where does the nuclear waste from these nuclear weapons go? Plans are under way to bury it in the Earth, dump it in the ocean, launch it into space, burn it into the Earth's atmosphere, "accidentally" spill it in a river or in the ocean or on the land, re-cycle it or just ignore it after it's been put in 50 gallon barrels or sitting in a nuclear submarine on a dock in Russia. (there are currently over 150 Russian nuclear submarines waiting to be disposed of). Russia has a terrible record of "spilling", the nuclear waste into rivers or the ocean or simply leaving it sitting around somewhere. Yet, they are offering to dispose of other county's nuclear waste for a price! In fact, nuclear waste disposal is already happening. America will lead the way to this tragedy! We are creating our own nuclear waste dump at Yucca Mountain, located near the Nevada "Test Site." How about those nuclear power plants that most countries have? The Three Mile Island radiation and iodine131 leak of 1979, the Chernobyl disaster of 1986 which released over a hundred times more fallout then the Hiroshima Atomic bomb and other "Radiation Leaks" have occurred on a regular basis. Are they polluting our air and water? Yes, and it's producing even more nuclear waste that mankind has no way to get rid of. It lasts for thousands and thousands of years!

UFO sightings have been reported for almost 100 years. These reports have come from numerous sources in America. From NASA astronauts and Air Force pilots, from U.S. Presidents and military leaders, these alien spacecraft have been seen and reported. Reports of UFOs have come from places all around the world, not just in America. But, only in America has the military made a conscious effort to both deny the existence of UFOs and cover up activity related to them. In 1941, prior to the first Atomic Bomb test, a "disc shaped space craft" with alien looking "hieroglyphic like" writing on it crashed near Cape Girardeau, Missouri. The alien spacecraft was recovered by FBI and military officials. Three alien bodies were also recovered that day."Three small alien bodies with large heads, large eyes and just a mere hint of a mouth were prayed over by The Reverend William Huffman, Pastor of the Red Star Baptist Church." The previous statement was part of a death bed statement made by the Reverend. He also stated he was sworn to secrecy by FBI and military. Did U.S. Military officials convince scientists to reverse engineer alien technology from this downed alien spacecraft? Reverse engineering is the secret military process of copying advanced technology from captured aircraft. Enemy weapons, propulsion systems, nuclear reactors, advanced computer systems and more are copied. Theoretically, hyper and warp drive technology, anti gravity propulsion and other advanced technology is copied and used to vastly improve our spacecraft and other secret weapons. Did reverse engineering of alien weapons and nuclear reactors help the U.S. develop the Atomic Bomb? Cape Girardeau is near Whiteman AFB, (Strategic Air Command Base and Strategic Missile Wing , ICBMs) and Scott AFB (headquarters for the entire Army Air Corp in 1941). Was this alien spacecraft spying on these U.S. Military installations when it crashed to Earth? Was it shot down while spying? The military denies it.

Is Mankind's reign on Earth coming to an end due to his greed and reckless behavior? Will Mankind's world wide pollution lead to global warming and the end of our beautiful planet Earth! Secret USAF investigations and their committees related to UFO reports have come to light. The Freedom of Information Act of July 4, 1966, 1996 and 2007 allowed access to secret Air Force files concerning UFOs. The Air Force had conducted several investigations into UFOs. These included: Project Sign, Project Blue Book and several others. In 1948, USAF Project Sign concluded that UFOs were not man made aircraft. Then in 1952 another Air Force investigation of UFOs, Project Blue Book, contradicted Project Sign, concluding that most UFO reports were either fake, mistaken for other aircraft or natural phenomenon. Earlier, in 1947 the

Air Force admitted that an alien spacecraft had been recovered in Roswell, New Mexico. Then the next day Air Force Brass contradicted themselves stating the UFO was actually a weather balloon. Then when NASA Astronaut Gordon Cooper reported a UFO sighting from his Mercury capsule while orbiting Earth people started believing they were real again. Did the Air Force play mind games with the American public over the UFO sightings? Most people think they did to cover up their own secret aircraft.

In Russia, China, Australia, all over the U.S., Pakistan, India, the Indian Ocean, North Korea, Algeria, all the oceans of the world, nuclear weapons testing has scarred the Earth. The U.S. tested nuclear weapons in Mississippi, Colorado, Alaska, Farmington, New Mexico (near Santa Fe) and Carlsbad, New Mexico! Three simultaneous detonations occurred in Rifle, Colorado of 30 kiloton bombs! These tests occurred above ground, under ground and at sea in places all around the world. There are some islands in the Pacific Ocean and other locations on land that are so "Hot" with radioactive fallout that no one can use them. Is there no end to Mankind's need for developing new and more deadly weapons that could destroy our world? This radioactive contamination lasts for thousands of years. Mankind and his insatiable appetite for power, conquest of other nations, greed and lust for material things is destroying our beautiful planet that took millions of years to evolve.

Man's need for energy from our planet's limited fossil fuels is also insatiable. With our fossil fuels becoming extinct, we are now polluting our planet with nuclear waste from hundreds of nuclear power plants all around the world. Will this radioactive pollution help create a world of global warming, polluted air and water? UFO sightings around the time of the first Atomic Bomb tests at the actual sites of these tests may have been a warning to mankind. "Trinity", it was called. Trinity was the first U.S. Atomic test detonation. How odd that the word Trinity would be used for this purpose when it is also the "Holy Trinity" in the Catholic Faith. This may have been closer to the truth than military brass had expected. We all may need the Holy Trinity before these weapons are finally destroyed and the threat of world wide destruction finally ended. Were these UFO sightings alien space craft or USAF secret aircraft? The USAF denies both!

In my book, "UFOs That Crashed to Earth", I take the reader through a series UFO sightings and investigations. The non stop excitement related to UFO sightings is real, not a fake or mistaken UFO report or a "Weather Balloon!" Unlike the USAF and our government, the lead characters find out the truth about UFOs and themselves. The enigma that the UFO phenomenon has become is finally resolved despite Air Force cover ups and harassment. Although a work of fiction, the story explores real

UFO reported sightings. This non stop mystery thriller is a must read for science fiction readers and anyone interested in the truth about "UFOs That Crashed to Earth."

Tom King
Author

Chapter 1:

Enlightenment

"I was falling down a bottomless pit to nowhere and then I saw Alice." "Alice in Wonderland?" "What's she doing in my dream?" Down, down, down I fell unable to stop, falling deeper and deeper into blackness." "Damn you all to hell Alice and screw the rabbit that's always in such a damned big hurry!" "I couldn't see her face, but it was Alice alright. Jake cursed them and his dream. "In my dream world it all seemed so real." THUDD!!! "I woke up when I hit the floor." "Ouch!!" "Damn it that hurt!" "I fell off the couch again damn it all to hell!" "I had passed out on the couch watching the idiot box and didn't know where the hell I was." "Then I remembered my messed up dream." "Jake Green R.I.P," was carved on my wooden tombstone up on Boot Hill in Dodge City, Kansas." "I was a low down, dirty, thieving scum who got strung up by a lynch mob for horse stealing." "Meanwhile, my turntable was playing the same damned song over and over." "He's a real nowhere man sitting in his nowhere land making all his nowhere plans for nobody." "He's as blind as he can be just sees what he wants to see nowhere man can you see me

9

at all." "Nowhere Man, that's me alright!" As the Sixties, Beatles song played over and over on his turntable, Jake recalled his real dilemma. He had finally reached the bottom of his pathetic life. Jake Green had tanked out and he was finished!

Jake Green woke up that morning from a very disturbing nightmare and realized his life was a total fraud! "Was it really just a dream?" "Maybe it was for real!" "I'm fifty years old and I have wasted all of my time being someone else." "What the hell have I really accomplished?" "Nothing, that's what!" "I have never had a creative or original thought in my head in all of my days on this planet!" "Hell, I've followed the leaders, played their little head games and done whatever was expected of me." Jake was really fed up with his life and wanted a change right now! He was all alone in this world after his life time sweetheart left him. "I'd like to kick myself right in my ass for that little screw up!" "I need to do something drastic to really shock myself out of this funk I'm in." "Something that will surprise even me the biggest cynic on Earth!" "I don't trust a damn soul on this planet." "Maybe I need to expand my horizons a little bit." "I think I'll leave Earth behind and find a better world." "Time to kick out the jams baby!"

Jake wondered just how he came to such a startling revelation. "Meditation." "That was it!" "No!" "The head shrink?" "I can't recall." Jake had tried all that before and it didn't do anything for him. "I know it wasn't drugs!" "At least not now anyway." "I guess I just woke up this morning and realized what a fake, piece of shit I really am." " I have no idea why or how I did it either." "I just know it's true."

Jake was born in New Hampshire. "The Live Free or Die State," was a good spot for him to grow up. He fooled around with sports and girls and then went to college. "I was a real wild man in high school and college." "Live free or die baby." "That was my motto!" "Only I got myself drafted three times and finally ended up in the damned United States Air Force." Jake told himself for the millionth time. "The "Air Farce" was really a pathetically out dated system, bureaucratically run by burnt out officers in a rigid caste system." "I survived it because I was in the air." "You know, Air Force flight duty on planes." "I was part of a medical evacuation team on C-130 transports." "In the air the military is different then on the ground." "No caste system exists in the air." "Everybody is on a first name bases." "There's no "yes sir" this or "no sir" that. Jake became a medic and was assigned to an aeromedical evacuation unit on C-130 transport planes in and around Vietnam. "It was 1970 and the damned Vietnam War was winding down and wouldn't end until a few more American GIs bought the farm." Jake recalled while sitting in his bedroom staring at the wall. "I was almost the 48,987[th] KIA of the "war," which wasn't really a war." "Since we never declared war on North Vietnam, it was a "conflict", not a "war." "So it was the Vietnam Conflict." "I got my leg blown apart and almost got killed in Nam in an "almost war!" "But "Killed in Action" still means you're dead, no matter where it is or what kind of war it is!" "What a way to go." "Pungi sticks to the throat or VC land mines blowing your ass up." "Shit, there were body bags all over the place." "Plus, all the wounded GIs were piling up." "We had our hands full evacuating the wounded out of Saigon to the states," Jake remembered with much disgust. "It was hectic as hell, but I loved it for some messed up reason." "I was actually doing something good for people in a war that nobody wanted anything to do with and I was getting flight pay!." "We had been taking a hell of a lot of wounded out of the bush around the border near Laos." "The 101 Air Mobile Division was taking a beating and had orders to pull out when it happened." Jake and his medical transport team were doing an emergency take off from the bush in VC territory when he was wounded. "The plane lifted almost straight up into the sky, but a VC mortar came tearing through the bottom hitting me." "They evacuated me to a Saigon Field Unit hospital." "I remember the "America" song, "Sandman", playing at the hospital. "Ain't it foggy outside, all the planes have been grounded." "Ain't the fire inside, let's all go and stand around it." "Well I understand you've been running from the man that goes by the name of the Sandman..." "Well I almost forgot to ask, did you hear of my enlistment." "Funny I've been there and you've been here and we ain't had no chance to drink that beer....." "I'll always remember that song." "I had gotten nailed with shrapnel and had emergency surgery." "The shrapnel had almost torn my damned leg off." Jake got a medical discharge from the military and settled in San Francisco. He got into the "60's" hippie scene and found a home at the Fillmore West concert hall. "After using a little too much acid and grass I bolted that scene and camped out in the Mojave Desert." "Finally, me and an old Air Force buddy started a business selling organic vegetables and fruit in San Francisco."

"It was pretty damned boring after what I did in the service." Jake told himself. "Going from a combat air evac medic in Nam to a grocery store clerk!" "What a bad trip!" "The business world sucks." "I needed something a lot more exciting." He told himself. "That was my biggest problem." "I was bored and felt burnt out all the time." "It was probably PTSD." Jake hung around California for awhile and played guitar in a few local bands. " I could never keep a rock band together." "Someone was always quitting." He gave it up and started writing music. "I recorded some tunes and got local San Francisco bands to play them." The Fillmore was rocking and he worked for Bill Graham who ran the rock shows. "I helped with the light shows and everything else." The rock scene died out and Jake went to live on a commune in the desert. After he realized how the lack of privacy made him feel he split."Screw those damned communes." Jake said out loud to no one. "They want all your

13

money and give you no privacy." "The babes were great, but I needed more freedom and couldn't stand feeling trapped all the time." "So here I am totally wasted" "Getting older and dumber everyday." "I've got lines on my damned face and I'm losing my memory." "I feel like shit warmed over." "Goodbye dead life and hello to life on the road."

"Right or wrong I'm hitting the road again." "Maybe out on the road I'll find myself." "I hope the hell I do someday real soon!" "First thing is to pack my shit into my van." Jake is a dreamer, not a planner. "I don't need to bother saying goodbye to anyone." "When you're a screw up and a fake you have no real friends." "I've got some fair weather, friends like most people." "But, they don't count." "Next, is to get my money from the damned bank." "Since I live in California and want to find myself, I will need to go East and then North." He said scheming. Jake had always been a schemer, not a planner. He never seemed to finish anything. He had good schemes, but rather poor, unrealistic plans. "I can't seem to get my act together!" He cursed as he stared at the wall in his pad. "I need help!" "I liked the people up there in the North and their country fried music." Jake still played Elvis albums. "I lived there once a long time ago and it was like being in a time machine." "They are still living in the fifties up there!" "That's my kind of scene." "Muscle cars, wife beater tee shirts, Marlboro's, greasers, drive in movies, country and western music and Saturday night barn dances."

"It's almost in Canada and that's alright with me!" It was the Spring of 1996 and Jake needed a major change. "Color me gone baby!"

Jake decided to take I-80 straight across the country. It was July and warm in California. But, once he got into the Mojave Desert it was cool at night. "One thing I always liked about the Mojave Desert is the spooky nights." He said to himself in a evil voice. "I mean you can see a long way off at night with the full moon shining down like a flood light." "And I can see all kinds of things moving around out there." "I have no idea what the hell they are." "It could be that I'm just getting too damned old and can't see for shit." He told himself with regrets. " Or maybe it's the acid I did as a hippie years ago." "You know, flashbacks." "They can come on you all of a sudden and you feel like you're tripping again." "Plus, the military has all these secret bases out here." "You know like Area 51." "So who the hell knows what's really happening out there." "I have no idea where the so called "Black Ops" places are." "I just know they are top secret." "The damned military isn't about to tell anyone about it." "But, if you happen on to one of them, look out you're busted by the guys in the white jeeps from Area 51!"

"Then there's the animals and whatever else is walking around out there." Jake was getting really excited about things these days. He was in limbo about his entire life. He wanted a normal life, but not a fake existence. "I have got to be me damn it!" "Whoever the hell that is!" He decided to stop and camp out near the highway. He set up his two man tent, got his sleeping bag and camping gear out of the van and started a fire with pieces of wood he found. "Now let's see." "Do I want Denny Moore Beef stew or Denny Moore Beef Stew?" Jake asked himself with a chuckle. "Think I'll have Denny Moore Beef Stew!" "Why the hell do I think that is so damned funny?" He was laughing hysterically. "I guess I already feel better." He put on some "Quicksilver Messenger Service" tunes on his eight track tape deck. The San Francisco band rocked on. "Who do you love, Who do you love?" " I've walked on 47 miles of barbed wire.. got a cobra skin for a neck tie, made out of rattle snack hide.. who do you love, who do you love?..." "I think I'll drink my bottle of cold duck to celebrate my new birth as a real person." Jake said licking his chops. He kept his camp fire going all night and slept out under the stars. "You can see the Milky Way as clear as can be." "Three's no pollution or smog to block it out here in the desert." "So, there's a lot of activity in the night sky." "That's the way I like it." "Think I'll smoke that last dubee I brought." "How the hell did I run out of smokes?" "I just don't have my priorities in order these day!" The "Eagles" were playing in the back ground on his eight track. "Yea I'm already gone and I'm feeling strong..." He lit up his last number and got really stoned. "Damn, this was good stuff." "I must have had it for about six months." "Can't even remember where I got it." "Suzie probably gave it to me." He got the munchies and ate a bunch of potato chips, two candy bars, drank three Bud cans of beer and the cold duck. Then he passed out from the pot.

Up before the crack of dawn Jake started out across the Mojave Desert in his "hippie" van. "I think I'm still a little wasted from that joint, ha, ha!" He laughed to himself. The van was a 1966 green VW panel van with Greatful Dead paintings and peace signs all over on the top and sides. "My freaking VW Van can go anywhere." "I love my VW!" He yelled to no one. He had a rug stapled down on the floor in case he got lucky with his woman."I've got pillows and a mattress too." "Yea baby!" "I've got twelve inch speakers all around and an eight track tape deck." "My car stereo kicks ass!" "I've got my Les Paul Guitar, an acoustic, my Fender Twin Amp and PA system." "You never know when you might find a rock band to jam with." "But, there's no freaking heater." "Why did the German's make a van with no heater?" "Isn't Germany cold in the Winter?" That question always bothered Jake.

It was chilly, pitch black and clear. He felt good and was ready to discover who he really was. Jake had been many things in his life. A high school jock, a college boy, a draftee, a business man and investor. All totally phony roles he played to earn money and other people's respect. He had a steady girl friend, but didn't know where she lived! "What the hell Suzie." "What is your special problem?" He asked himself with self doubts. "Maybe I just don't turn her on anymore." "It can happen to an old fart like me." "Maybe she thinks I can't get it up!" "Well, I know I can!" "Anybody who thinks Jake Green is a sexless, lifeless piece of crap is full of shit!" "Wait till I see that woman." "I'll get her to come on to me for a change." "That's it." "I'll play hard to get and she'll try to make out with me for a change!" "I'll just act ho hum about it." He said with great self satisfaction. "I have a plan that will make her crave me." "Ah huh!" "You brilliant stud Jake!"

Now he was just living one day at a time and blending in with the background. He planned to simply observe things and people. That way maybe he'd find himself. "If I live for the moment and stay in the present I'll see who I am." He told himself.

A bright light suddenly flashed in his face. "What the hell was that!!" Jake had just seen a very bright flash of orange-red light streak past just above his head. "Now I've seen everything!" "A freaking UFO!!" All of a sudden the thing came back and almost took the top of the van off. He stopped, got out and watched as it sped away straight up into the black, desert sky. "If I live to be a hundred I will never see anything like that again!" Suddenly, two air force jets came speeding right at him. There was no sound until they were right on him. Thunder echoed across the desert. The F-106 Delta darts kicked in their after burners as they climbed up into the early morning desert sky in pursuit of the UFO. "That looks a lot like a rocket being fired from the lead F-106." Jake yelled to no one. Suddenly the sky lit up with a huge yellow blast." Something or someone was just hit and is falling down to Earth." As he watched in stunned silence, four more jets appeared and shook the desert floor as they kicked in their after burners. As the ground vibrated from the sonic blasts of the sound barrier being broken, Jake covered his ears with his hands and stared up into the sky. The entire sky over his head was on fire with pieces of debris falling to Earth. "I can see tons of stuff falling to the desert floor over there!" He yelled at the desert sky. "Holy shit!" "The damned UFO was shot down!"

"I think I'll try to drive over there where the explosion was." He told himself between excited breaths. He jumped into the van and headed straight across the desert towards the area all lighted up. "No doubt I'll be met by the security police or something." He said out loud. Some jet choppers flew by and Jake heard more explosions ahead. "I'll stop and get my camera out and snap a few pictures off." As he took several pictures he grabbed the bottle of Jim Beam whiskey in the back seat and took a long drink. "I've got to steady my nerves." He promised himself. "This may only happen once in a lifetime and I've got of make the most of it." "Besides, I want to know if the Air Force really did cover up UFO sightings like at Roswell."

As he approached the site of the explosion he noticed something on fire on the ground up ahead. "I can't quite make it out and don't have my binoculars." "I wonder how close they'll let me get." Now he could see what appeared to be a huge disk shaped, shiny, spacecraft. "It has to be at least 200 feet long and really large in circumference. He stopped and snapped more pictures and proceed to the wreck. "I can see some kind of markings on the side of the alien space craft." It was a design he didn't recognize. Several soldiers jumped from the chopper and ran towards the alien looking space craft. They began covering it with a tarp and netting material. But, it was so large and so damaged that it would take awhile to cover it all up. "That gives me time to get some close ups." Jake said out loud in a nervous voice. He began loading film in the camera and snapping off shots. The smoke and fire coming from the UFO obscured the view at times depending on the wind. "Why the hell don't they put the fire out!" The breeze was igniting the blaze and a huge fire covered the object. Finally, some men wearing white fire proof suits began using foam to put out the fire. "Damn that stinks!" Jake held his nose. Now the space craft was covered with white foam. Next more men appeared with white suits on and were trying to get inside the UFO. "How the hell do they know where the door is?" Jake wanted to yell at them, but decided to shut up. Apparently one of them knew how to gain entry because they were interring the space craft from the top. "Holy shit almighty!!" Jake screamed. The alien spacecraft started to move and looked like it was going to take off. As parts of it blew up and flew off in all directions the men started jumping out and running away from it.

It was like the dying, last gasp of a huge whale or something. Finally, the monster, UFO stopped moving and appeared dead. "We killed another one!!" Jake yelled into the sky.

By now it was completely light out and the sun was coming up. "They'll probably load pieces of the damn thing onto huge trucks or something and cart it away." Jake decided to get the hell out of there right away. He turned the van around and drove off as fast as he could. He took a couple more pulls from the Jim Beam and began laughing. "What the hell am I doing out here?" "I can get arrested and never be heard from again!" "I can see the headline now." "It will read: "Jake Green arrested for spying at top secret Air Force instillation in the desert." "He was locked up at an undisclosed location." "He has not been seen or heard from in over 10 years." "No one will even notice I'm gone because I didn't ever say goodbye to anyone!" He said to himself cursing. "This is freaking great!" He decided to pull off the road and try to blend in with some tourists. He was about ten miles from the crash site and at a resort called the "Mojave Inn and Casino." He went into the bar and asked about a room. He had hidden the van under some trees and it looked safe for now. "I'll stay here for a few days and mellow out." He promised himself.

Jake had time to research the alien, UFO crashes in the area on a computer at the Inn. The first one reported from around the U.S. was the "Cape Girardeau Missouri Crash" of 1941. "They covered that one up by silencing a whole town!"

Jake figured. "But, the Reverend who was called in by local police for a "funeral" of the dead aliens, later made a death bed statement." "He reported that a disc shaped UFO crashed and alien bodies and the alien spacecraft were recovered by the FBI and military." "He said that police and FBI agents were at the scene of the crash." "The list of alien, UFO crashes goes on and on." "They were: Socorro, NM 5-31-47, Roswell 7-7-47, San Augustin, NM 7-5-47, New Mexico desert 8-13-47, Paradise Valley, AZ 10-47, Aztec, NM 2-13-48 and 4-48, Hart Canyon near Aztec on 3-25-48, (two alien space craft were found and 17 alien bodies recovered.) White Sands, NM 3-25-48, Mojave Desert, Cal. 1-50, Carson Sink, Nev. 7-24-52, (2 pilots saw 3 UFOs in a V formation with delta wing airfoils), Otis AFB Falmouth, MA. (Air Force pilots chased a UFO and had to eject, Air Force plane was never found)." "And there are tons more all over the Earth!"

"The Reverse Engineering of alien technology theory is that the U.S. has copied alien technology concerning radar, propulsion systems, navigation systems, life support, communication, weapons, stealth, computer chips and nuclear power and weapons." Jake had read about this on the computer and it explained the theory. "When UFOs landed the military took all the debris to a secret lab called "Hanger 18" at Wright Paterson Air Force Base in Ohio." "They pieced it all back together and then examined it." "If they could copy a part or machine they did." Jake kept reading. "We've been using reverse engineering for years on German

WW11 rockets, jet planes and other Nazi high tech weapons." "That's how we got our first rockets." The German V2 rocket was copied and used by America." "It led to the more powerful Atlas rockets and the ICBM's" "It was just a matter of copying someone else's technology," "So, we did it with the alien UFOs too." Jake concluded. "It's all here to read." "It is very believable too!" Jake said with great enthusiasm. "It's all in the reports and they can't deny all of it." Jake felt he was really on to something now and ready to launch a new career as a new reporter.

"Then there was the Shag Harbour Incident of October 1967 in Nova Scotia, Canada." "U.S. Authorities helped cover that one up too." "It's all documented by Canadian authorities that a UFO crashed into Shag Harbour and the UFO debris was found by Navy divers." "And last but not least the big one!" "The Washington DC UFO Incident of July, 1952. "Seven UFOs were picked up on radar by air traffic controllers at Washington National Airport and at Andrews AFB ten miles away." "They reported radical movements of the alien spacecraft and stated it could not be USAF jets." " An airline , DC-4 pilot on take off also sighted the UFOs." "The headline in the paper read: "Saucers Swarm Over Capital." "These UFOs were seen for a two week period." "Major Gordon Cooper reported a UFO approaching his Mercury Capsule while on his last of 22 orbits of Earth on 5-15-63." "He described it as a glowing object." "The Nazi's actually built a disc shaped spacecraft that was 25 meters in diameter and traveled at a rate of speed of 4800 K.M. Per hour." "The "Haunebu 1" held eight men and had electri-magnetic engines which used Earth's gravity for propulsion," "They can't deny everything that has ever fucking happened!" Jake yelled to himself. "There is way too much evidence of alien, UFO crashes and sightings for the Air Force to delete it all." "Even their huge propaganda machine can't cover it all up!" Jake was ready to get going with his new career and he kept reading from the files.

"Project Sign", was created by the USAF in 1948 to investigate UFOs and determine if they were a threat to national security." "The conclusion was that UFOs are alien space craft and not man made." "General Nathan Tining of Wright Paterson AFB led the investigation." "He coined the phrase "Unidentified Flying Object." "That's where Hanger 18 was!" Jake told himself. "Later in 1952 President Truman ordered the creation of "Project Blue Book" to debunk Project Sign." "They investigated over 12,000 UFO sightings and concluded most of them were faked, Air Force jets mistaken for UFOs or natural phenomenon.." "Captain Edward J. Ruppelt headed that project." "Lastly, was "Majestic 12", a committee of scientists, military and government officials created to cover up UFO sightings." "The Air Force denied it existed!" "Project Grudge was then created to debunk these same UFO sightings." After reading all of the documented cases of UFO sightings Jake was convinced they existed and that the Air Force was covering them up.

Amazingly, no Air Force security came around to look for him. "I'm starting to wonder why." He asked himself. There was nothing in the local paper or on the news about the crash or the pursuit of the UFO by the Air Force jets. "Maybe I'll go nose around out there." Jake told himself. "But first I'll get rid of the van and rent some other FBI looking car." "You know." "A black, four door Ford or something." Jake mumbled to himself. "I can bring the van to a body shop and get it painted while I drive the rented car." He was scheming again. Jake drove over to Needles and dropped the van off for a paint job and rented a four door, black Ford sedan. "This will be my official "FBI agent's car." As he studied his map he realized how close the crash was to Edwards Air Force Base. "That's how those jets got there so fast." "I'll pack up the car with a cooler, ice, lots of cans of Bud, a shit load of ham and cheese, bread, and stuff and Jim Beam whiskey." "I'll drive by night with no headlights on and camp out during the day." "One last detail." "I've got to buy a dark, navy blue suit and white shirt and tie." 'Hell, I'll blend right in with the Feds." Jake said to himself laughing.

It was about half a day back to the crash sight and he left at 8pm from Needles. As he drove along he thought to himself, "what a strange town Needles is." "It's like everybody is just walking around in a daze." "Who the hell would want to live there?" "It's in the middle of the desert and hundreds of miles from any city or civilization." "I've got to look into this some more later." It was a clear night and the moon was out and bright. It would be easy to find the crash sight and still have some hours of darkness left. "I'll stash the car and walk to the crash site." As he approached the crash site he saw flashing red lights. "It looks like a trailer truck on it's side right where the UFO was." Jake said to himself. Local police were motioning cars to move along and not stop to look. There was no evidence of a crashed UFO and Jake wasn't surprised. "They staged a fake truck accident to cover up the UFO evidence." "I wonder where they took it." "Probably to Hanger 18 at Wright-Patterson Air Force base near Dayton, Ohio." He told himself. "How ironic that the base is named after the Wright Brothers and they are using it for secret UFOs." "From balsa wood bi-planes to UFO, Star Trek space ships!" Jake drove off shaking his head.

"What the hell I might as well check it out, I'm going that way anyhow." "There must be some way I can find out where they brought the damn thing." Since he was so close to Edwards, Jake decided to swing by and look for any evidence of the alien spacecraft. "I'll do the "visitor" routine and snoop around the base." He changed into some shorts and a surfer shirt and sandals to look like a California tourist. Then he went to the base, requested a visitor pass and went in. Edwards Air Force Base is this sprawling place where a lot of new Air Force jets are tested. "The problem is I don't know where to start looking." "Let's see." "If I had to hide a huge alien spacecraft where would

I put it?" "Hanger 18 of course!" "But, that's not here." "They must have some huge hangers here though." He asked some airmen where the large hangers are and they actually told him. "Ah, hah!" "That's the one." He told himself as he stared at a huge hanger. "They won't let me anywhere near it." So, he decided to get a coffee and just sit a little ways off and watch and see if there was any suspicious activity. After about three hours he was ready to give up and go home when a group of Air Force brass drove up to the hanger. They all went inside and didn't come out.

CHAPTER 2:

THE AIR FORCE COVER UPS

"Smuggled lots of smokes from folks in Mexico, get baked by the sun every time I go to Mexico. I've been whipped by the rain driven by the snow I'm drunk and dirty don't you know that I'm still willin. And I've been kicked by the wind robbed by the sleet had my head stoved in but I'm still on my feet and I'm still willing....." "That sounds like me." Jake told himself as the "Little Feet" song played on his tape deck. "That Air Force Project Sign really bothers me a lot." "They admitted the damned UFOs were not man made and then covered it all up." "Why bother with such a huge undertaking?" Jake asked himself as he drove along. "The secret Air Force Bases and all the top secret aircraft must have been the reason." "That means they'll do anything to keep it a secret." "That means anything!"

"These bastards will kill people or abduct them to silence them for good!" "If there really are alien abductions it's probably the damned military that's doing it!" "Make it look like the people abducted are wacko or crazy." "Make them blame it on aliens!" Jake said to himself shaking his head.

"Then the press can make fun of the victims and make them out to be fools." "I wouldn't doubt it if the media was in on the whole damned cover up." "And those crop circles." "That's probably the military doing that too!" "It's all a damned big game they play to confuse the real issues." "Now I'm getting paranoid again." "I've got to stop thinking about it."

Jake's old Air Force experience would come in handy in the very near future. "I got Drafted into the army, but then enlisted in the USAF." He told himself. "Good old Vietnam!" But, I was a damned medic, not a pilot!" "So, how the hell do I know where the damned Air Force hides UFOs!?" "Hurry up and wait!" "That's the stupid Air Force motto!" "So, my experience in the Air Force tells me to be patient." Jake was asking himself what else the Air Force Brass could be looking at except the recovered alien spacecraft when the huge hanger doors began opening. He saw it! "I can see a large pile of shiny metal and other debris." He said while speaking into a tiny tape recorder. "Now I can see what appears to be the top of the alien spacecraft." As the doors began to close Jake decided to leave for now. He would find a motel in nearby California City and rest up. It would take awhile to check this situation out and investigate.

When he checked into the Mojo Inn he thought he recognized a motor cycle in the parking lot. It was a BMW 650 with a skull and crossbones on the back fender. It was all chrome and in mint condition. The bike could only belong to one person. Suzie "Beamer" Brooks. Jake had a scheme. He would go see her and act all official and not all turned on. "I'll do the old hard to get routine." He said to himself with an evil grin on his satisfied face. "I wonder what in the hell she's doing here." "It figures she'd be here right now after she took off on me last month." He would knock on her door and find out. After he checked into his room and put his things away he went over and banged on her door. This half dressed, blond headed beauty with closed, sleepy eyes opened the door. "Suzie!" Jake yelled with a laughing sound. "What....." "Jake is that you?" He grabbed her and gave her a big hug and hauled off and kissed her. "Why you cute little thing." "Where have you been hanging out anyway?" "Come on in Jake and sit a spell." "Don't mind if I do." They cracked open some cans of Bud and yucked it up about old times gone by. Jake and Suzie had known each other since high school in Fairfield in the sixties. Since it was 1996 and they were thirty years older, they appreciated each other more then ever. "God, you look good enough to eat girl." "I think I'll stick around for awhile and see what comes up!" "Sorry Jakester." "I have to head out in the morn." "Oh come on honey I was just pulling your leg." "I know, but I have to meet someone in Yucca Valley tomorrow." "But, we've got tonight and the night is young my man." "Sounds like a plan and I just happen to have some more beers and a bottle of Jim Beam in the car." "Is that Ford sedan your car?" "I thought you only drove VW Panel Vans?" "I do honey and it's a long story." Jake went to get the booze and stuff and took a quick shower. "I guess my plan is shit." "I can't resist the damned girl!" He told himself with disgust. While he was gone Suzie changed into shorts and sexy lingerie. "Wow!" Jake moaned when he returned. "My goodness you look so beautiful." Suzie is this five foot, sex inch blond with a rather beautiful body. She speaks in this cute and affectionate voice. "Since she is a dancer, she knows how to shake her booty." Jake told himself with hopeful expectations. After they had some of her smokes and told some jokes Jake asked her who she was meeting in Yucca Valley. "It's a business deal and you can't go with me." "I'm selling the bike for $50,000 to a dealer." "How are you going to get home after the sale?" "I was planning to take the bus back to Fairfield." "Listen honey why don't I just follow you and we'll hang out for a few days." "Jake are you sure of that?" "It doesn't sound like the Jake Green I know to stay with one woman for more than one night." "Hell girl you left me remember?" "Yea, I needed some space." "But, I'm damn glad to see you honey." "You gona break my heart again babe?" Jake asked her. " No way honey." "Alright then honey." "Now let's get some sleep."

Suzie woke Jake up a 5am and headed out to Yucca Valley. She knew some back road short cuts through Adelanto near George Air Force Base and down into Apple Valley and on into Landers. When they got to Yucca Valley it was noon and after the deal was closed they went to Twenty Nine

Palms and had lunch. As they sat and ate at an outdoor Mex cafe Jake told her about the crashed UFO. "Look Jake you can't really be serious about chasing after UfOs." "Give it up man." "Oh come on baby what else do we have to do." "You can be my partner FBI agent." "I'll buy you a navy blue suit and white dress shirt with brown dress heels." "I might even thrown in some lingerie baby!" "Well in that case, alright." "But only for a few days you character."

When they arrived at Edwards Air Force Base where the UFO had been the hanger was empty. After snooping around they found out that a C-5 Galaxy transport had landed and taken off at 6am. It was listed as destination secret. They had hit a dead end. "Now what your brilliance?" Suzie asked sarcastically. "I don't actually know." "I'll have to think on it for a spell." Jake said scratching his head. "How many places are there for the Air Force to take these things?" "Listen Jake I wasn't going to say anything cause I personally think you're crazy, but remember when we drove past George AFB?" "Yea, I do and so what?" "Well I saw a C5 Galaxy landing." "It may not be anything at all though." "Or it could be where the damn alien spacecraft is." Jake said excitedly. "I know some people in Victorville and I can bring you there." She told him. "You got it and that's it honey." "Color us gone baby." "Okay, Jake good enough for now." They were still dressed in their "FBI" suits and figured they would go nose around at George AFB and then go over to Victorville. "Sure enough there's the C5 transport honey." "It's near a building and the flight line, see it?" "Yea and now what?" "We'll just sit here and watch." "Get the camera and my new binoculars baby." They munched on french fries and drank a bottle of Strawberry Hill wine. It was getting dark and cold. "We may as well go over to Victorville honey." Jake said. "That's okay with me." Suzie said. "What the hell can we see in the dark anyway." "Jake said. It was only five miles to Victorville and when they arrived there were cops all over the place. "It looks like a swat team convention!" "What the hell is going on here?" Jake yelled at the cops. "Just move on sir." The security police yelled to him. "We can park the car and walk around in back to my friends house." Suzie said. They parked the "FBI" car and made it to the friends house in about ten minutes. They weren't there, but Suzie found the key and got them in. "Well, we're safe for now." She told Jake. "Look here baby." "I brought the bottle of Jim Beam." "Sounds good to me." She replied. After a long night of drinking and love making they decided to stick around at the house and wait for Suzie's friends to get home.

"You know Jake I think I still love you." "Now don't get all chocked up or anything." "Your the first person I ever said that to and probably the last." "I love you too baby and I always have." He told her and they went back to bed. Suzie and Jake were like "Batman and Bat Woman." They really worked well together and had a lot of fun. "Listen, remember the time we sneaked into that old mansion in Vacaville near the prison?" "Of course I do honey." Jake said to his lover. "We were scared shit less." "Suzie said. "Well, I've got a confession to make." "Really?" Jake said to her. "Yea." "I wanted to make it with you that night." "I never realized that honey." "You were such a tomboy." "Yea and I was afraid you were turned off by me." "That could never happen baby," Jake told her. "Anyway, when we heard that creaking noise and saw a light in the basement we ran like hell." Suzie said laughing. "That kind of put the kabosh to that idea!" "Yea" Jake said with a questioning voice. "You really felt that way babe?" "Don't let it go to your head you big cretin!" "I never played football, but I could have won the 100 yard dash that night." Jake said laughing. "That's okay with me Jake." "I still love your dumb hippie ass." "Well, I'm a changed man now baby." "I've got an FBI car and suit." "Plus, I'm rich." "Yea, Jake how did you get all that money you saved up?" "I invested in computers and computer chips, and made a killing in the stock market." "Yea right!" "You probably grew some home grown pot and made a big sale like in Easy Rider." "Okay baby whatever you say." "So where are we going next Jake?" "We'll wait until the heat is off around here and go back out to the base."

In the morning they wrote a note to Suzie's friends and headed out. When they arrived at the same place they had been before, a huge crane was lifting something into the air near the C5. "It looks like their trying to re-assemble the UFO." "That's what the FAA does after a plane crash." Suzie said. "My girlfriend at Travis AFB is in the FAA and she told me how they do it." "They take each little piece of debris and match it up with the other parts until they have the complete plane." "That's it Suzie!" Jake yelled. "That's how they figured out how to reverse engineer alien spacecraft." "They copy what the FAA does after a plane crashes." "It's a logical next step." "Yea that's right." Suzie said. "My friend told me they have the actual blueprints or schematics of the plane they are trying to re-assemble to use as a guide." "We just figured out how the Air Force reverse engineers alien spacecraft and re-creates the more advanced spacecraft they recovered from an alien UFO crash site!" "Only they don't have the blueprints Jake." "They have no way to guide themselves while trying to re-create an alien spacecraft." Suzie said. "How do you know that baby?" "Maybe the blueprints are inside the UFO somewhere." That's a awfully big leap in logic Jake." "Maybe it is." "It sure sounds like the Air Force I have learned to hate." Jake said.

"It's too bad we don't have a telephoto lens for the camera." Jake said. "We're too damn far away." He said to her in a frustrated voice. "Listen, how about if I drive over there and tell them I'm lost and ask for directions." Suzie suggested. "I'll bring the camera and snap a few off." "Okay baby and don't get caught." "I don't want to get my "FBI" car impounded!" "Plus, I just discovered that you and me have a whole lot in common and a whole new career in news reporting, or something like it." "Okay Jakester." "Yea and baby, I don't want to lose you again!"Jake told her and really meant it.

She drove over to the huge crane as Jake watched from the fence. As she drove up to them they ran out to meet her and took her out of the car. "I can see them talking with her now." "Alright!" Jake said excitedly. "They are letting her go." Jake said to himself. As she drove up to Jake he was very relieved and realized how much her cared for her. "Honey, what happened?" "Jake, they questioned me and told me I was trespassing on federal property and could go to jail." "But, it was after I snapped one off!" "Alright baby." "My brave baby." "You did very good." Jake grabbed her and kissed her long and hard on the lips. "Let's go get these pictures of the alien spacecraft developed." Jake said while looking at the Air Force base behind him. As they walked off a huge black jet was taking off. It looked like a flying wing or spacecraft as it kicked in the after burners and tore up the morning sky. It suddenly disappeared into space. "Let's get the hell out of here!" Jake yelled to Suzie.

They decided to drive over to Victorville and then on into LA. The cops in Victorville had cleared out, but there still was no one home at Suzie's friend's house. "That was damned strange." "All those security police the other night." Jake seemed puzzled. "I don't get it." "Why send all those cops here?" "I know what your thinking and you're paranoid!" Suzie yelled to him. "How can you say I'm freaking out when we could have been followed?" "Because, they couldn't have known where we were going!" "Come on Jake, get a grip!" "Alright." "I guess I am a little paranoid." "A little paranoid!" "You're ready for the padded cell at the state hospital!" "Those cops were here because of base security." "Someone must have escaped or something." Suzie told Jake in a sarcastic way. "It's a top secret project Jake!" "Okay baby you're right." Jake said. "You're damned right I'm right!" She said laughing. "I guess that sounded a little off color." "A little off color!" "You're ready for a padded cell!" "Okay you made your point numb nuts!" As they spoke to one another a white Jeep drove by the house. "Okay Major Armstrong we're keeping an eye on Green and the woman." "Yes sir we'll stay put." "Over and out."

At the LA underground you can get anything done cheap. The film was developed in one hour and they headed back into the desert. "It's an alien spacecraft alright." Suzie said with surprise as she looked at the pictures. "I really thought you had lost your mind Jake." "So now that we have the pictures what do we do with them?" "Nobody will believe we actually saw a real UFO." "I know." "That's why we have to get more proof." Jake said. "I 'm going to mail the negatives to a friend first though." "Then we'll head for Area 51." "Why go there?" "That's so closely guarded we won't get within miles of it." Suzie said. "That's where they test all new jets and aircraft." "So that's where they'll test the spacecraft if they can reverse engineer it." Jake said while trying to find Groom Lake on the map.

They took I-15 out of LA to route 93 to route 375 to Rachel, Nevada. From there it's back roads and travel by night to Area 51. "How do you like the "Extraterrestrial" Highway baby?" "You are joking right?" "There are so many Air Force test sites out here that you can't possibly know what's really going on." Jake told her. "How can they just flat out deny every damn UFO sighting?" "There is a test site over at Tonopah where they test nukes and ICBM's" "Then over at Indian Springs AFB where all the new stuff is tested." "And of course Nellis AFB the biggest one of all." "They have secret under ground test sites and jet propulsion labs too." "It's a maze of "UFO" and secret military weapons." "Okay, Jake so here we are." "Now what the hell are we doing?" "I don't know baby." "Let me think on it."

They set up their camp site near the highway. "The Air Force is developing new spacecraft and flying them." "But, they don't have the alien technology correct and the damn things crash." "So how can they perfect it?" Suzie asked. "They copy alien spacecraft that they capture!" "I can't see a damn thing it's so dark Jake." "That's my theory." "How can you prove it Jake?" Suzie asked him with some degree of frustration and disbelief. Jake didn't have an answer. It was pitch dark and the desert was completely still. "What the hell have you gotten me into?" "I've got a really bad feeling about this." Suzie said while shaking from the cold desert night air. "Yea it is a little creepy." Jake had to admit. "I know it's crazy baby, but hang in there a little longer and I'll take you out on the town." "Is that a promise you big lug!" "Yes it is." "What the hell." "In for a penny in for a pound." She said laughing. "Maybe we'll get lucky and see something tonight." "We better Mr. Spock!" "In the morning the place will be crawling with those white Jeeps and secret agents!" Suzie said sarcastically. They got a fire going and set up the tent. "I figure we may as well have a fire." "If they catch us we'll say we got lost." "That fire feels really good." "I may never get warm again." Suzie said while trying to warm herself from the heat by the fire. "Get the steaks and beer out baby and prepare for a feast." As they cooked out and drank beer and laughed they didn't know they were being watched. There were listening posts near them and a white Jeep sat on a hill nearby.

After several days of waiting for something to happen they got bored and restless. They decided to head over to Hiko where there is a ghost town. "Three days of sitting in this sun is enough for me." Jake said. "How about a ghost town baby?" "Anything except where we are." She said. As they drove into Hiko on route 318 near Ash Springs they seemed to sense something strange. When they finally arrived in the ghost town it appeared to be a bizarre scene right out of a fifties horror movie. "It's like "The Werewolf" with Lon Chaney or something." Jake said. "No, it's more like Jake Green and his dumb broad girlfriend!" "Oh come on baby this is so cool." "There's a full moon too." "Jake shut up you cretin!" "I'm all for leaving while we still can." Suzie said. "It's perfect." Jake said laughing. "Do I remind you of a freaking werewolf or something?" "Yea sometimes you do." "It's not too cool here Jake!" "I'm scared." "Do you feel that cold wind baby?" "Yea, Jake maybe we better leave." "No baby we're on vacation from Area 51." "There is like no one really living here." "So let's just camp out near that old barroom over there." "This goin be fun!!" Jake screamed to no one. They set up camp and toured the ghost town.

"A few ranchers are still around I guess." "But. It's pretty much abandoned." Jake said. After checking the few remaining buildings out they went into the barroom. "The Silver Dollar Saloon." Jake said laughing. "Why are these ghost town bars always called the "Silver Dollar?" Suzie asked. "It was probably a silver mine town before it went bust." Jake said. They both had a shot of Jim Beam at the dusty bar. "There's some old pictures over here Jake." "This one looks like you my man." "Maybe it's my great, great grandfather." Jake said laughing. "No, I mean it Jake." "It really is you." "Let me see that." She handed the picture to Jake. "Damn it is me!" "This is really strange." Suzie said. "Yea, it's Twilight Zone material." They looked around and couldn't find much else of any interest, so they went back to the camp site to get a fire going. "What will it be baby, steaks or steaks?" Jake asked laughing. "I'll take a lobster!" She answered. "Sorry we're in the desert, no sea food."

After dark the place was even more creepy. "What was that creaking noise over at the barroom?" "Oh probably only the "Psycho Miner." Jake said. "Don't do that you mental case!" "It was the wind and that's all." Jake said laughing. "I could swear I saw some one running into the shack over there." She said. "Here have a belt of whiskey." When they finally fell asleep several dark figures were lurking nearby. The big guy in charge said, "let's get back to the Jeeps men." "Green and company are just camping over here." "I hope Green liked the photo of himself we planted in the barroom." "Yea, that should freak them out!" "Let's move out men." "Yea Bob we'll take care of them later." "Back to base camp men." "Yes sir Major Armstrong."

Suzie woke up and rolled over to kiss Jake. He was gone. "Jake!" "Where the hell are you!" She got up and looked all around. About a half an hour later she saw him walking around near the Silver Dollar Bar. "Jake get over here!" "Okay baby." "Where the hell have you been Jake?" "Snooping around." "That's what I do for a living now baby." "Well, start snooping with me buster!" "Okay baby." "Did you see anything?" She asked. "I think someone still lives around here I saw tire tracks over behind the far building." He said. "But, who the hell really knows?" "Let's face it Jake your UFOs could be anywhere out here." "Yea, you are right on." "That's why we have to be patient." "Let's head back where we were near Area 51 for a couple more nights." "Well, at least there were no real ghosts here last night." Suzie said. "Hey, that's right baby!" "So let's think positive." "Jake, why was there a picture of you in the barroom?" "I wish I knew." "It may have been someone that just looked like me." When they arrived at the camp site near Bald Mountain Jake noticed some new tire marks in the sand. "See this baby." "They've been here." "So stay alert."

They watched and listened for the day and got their camp fire going right before dark. "Wanna smoke my last number?" Suzie asked Jake. "Does the sun come up every morning and do zebras have stripes?" Jake answered. "I take that to be a yes!" Suzie said sarcastically. As the sun came up the next morning and Jake crawled out of his sleeping bag, Suzie moaned, "well that was worth it!" "Relax baby I've got a plan that can't lose." "We'll just get visitors passes to Nellis AFB." "Or maybe just call one of those UFO experts on the Discovery Channel." "We know the Air Force is hiding the damn UFO things some where out here." What the hell, if they can fake the moon landings they can do anything!" Jake said in gesture. Suzie gave him a punch and said, "you big clown." She was laughing her fool head off and Jake was too. "Okay honey you win let's get the hell out of here." Jake finally came down to earth. "Can we get rid of this damned "FBI" car please?" "Okay baby you're on."

Jake drove Suzie home and she planned to go back to work as a "dancer" in strip joints. But, as they drove away from Area 51 workmen were busy piecing together fragments of the alien spacecraft.

It was under ground and away from prying eyes. "Hey Ralph what the hell do you imagine this is?" The Air Force investigator held up an alien looking generator. "How about this Jim?" The engineer pointed to a bizarre looking clock. "By the way Ralph where did they put the alien bodies?" "Down in the deep freeze like usual." "Do you think this thing will ever fly again?" "Why not some of the others did." "How the hell do you think we copied them and developed the stealth?" "We had to fly the damn things." As the workmen continued piecing together the damaged alien spacecraft Jake and Suzie drove away from Area 51. They would be back!

CHAPTER 3:

BEST JOB IN THE WHOLE WORLD

Jake was on a real roll. He had seen the Air Force shoot down a UFO which turned out to be an alien spacecraft and and he had pictures of it. But, he was running out of money fast. It was time for him to get back to work and earn some money. Since he had retired from the business world and had no job, he had to create one. Jake loved photography and writing so, he decided on a career in photo journalism, reporting and song writing."I'm a free spirit, free lance photag and reporter." "The song writing comes natural when I play guitar." Jake told himself all this and was off and running as usual when he got an idea in his head. "I'll set up shop somewhere in the desert and start covering every report of UFOs and other bizarre things." "I'll interview some UFO experts and Area 51 workers." "This goin be funnnn!!"

The problem for Jake is that in the desert there really isn't much news to report or anything to take photos of. That would present a problem for most people, but not Jake. He would create his own news. So, he started bringing his photos of the crashed UFO into the local newspapers. He went to, or contacted, the Victorville Daily Press, California City News, Mojave Desert News, The Union, Apple Valley News, Rosamond Local News, Antelope Valley Press, Lancaster Local News, Barstow Desert Dispatch and Local News, Needles Desert Star and Local News, LA Times, San Francisco Chronicle and New York Times. He also contacted National Geographic, Playboy, Men's Journal, Texas Monthly, Newsweek, Time, CBS, NBC, ABC, TBS, CNN, MSNBC, Larry King, National Inquirer, People Mag., BBC, Moscow Times, London Times, The Nome Nugget, Fairbanks Daily News, Whitehorse Star, Atlanta Journal Constitution and more. Whether any of these "media outlets" would ever pay any attention to him was another thing. He couldn't worry about that. Jake figured he'd end up in Alaska or the Yukon Territory someday so he included them.

Sure enough and to his great surprise articles started appearing in these various papers and on TV. The general theme of the reports was that Jake was a crazy guy who made it all up. But, one newspaper ran with the story. The "Yucca Mountain Nuclear Repository Monthly", believed his story and sent their reporter to interview him. Jake had been camping in the desert near Area 51 and was interviewed there. Jerry Coolwater from the paper showed up one night at Jake's campfire. "Sir, may I speak to you about the alien spacecraft?" "How the hell did you find me?" "Sir, I knew where you were from Air Force surveillance cameras which I have access to from the waste dump." "No way buddy." "Your a fake!" "No sir I am not." Okay, so why do you care about the alien space craft that the Air Force shot down?" "It's news worthy." Jake was getting pissed off. "Do you know you're the only reporter that's showed up or contacted me." "I have a website too and it's dead." "Well yes sir." "That's the way they fixed it." "Who's they?" "The US. Military and FBI." "You may see some white jeeps around here very soon." Jerry said. "Anyway how did you first find out about the Air Force UFO project?" "What!?" "The project?" "What project!?" "Oh, I thought you knew and so do the FBI." Jake was really confused now. "No, I had no idea about any secret project and it was an accident that I ever saw the damn UFO to begin with." "You are in big trouble Jake." "They're going to be coming for you." "If what your saying is true you better clear out and not come back." Jerry was getting ready to take off. "They're watching you closely." As he drove away Jake laughed and said, "ta hell with them!"

He figured that since they were watching him he may as well go all the way. "I'll transmit the photos to the London Times and the BBC." He set up his computer at a motel and emailed it all. After weeks of frustration and never getting anywhere he got desperate. "I'll have to take a different approach to this." He told himself. He was on his way back to Area 51 when it finally happened. "I wonder what that state trooper wants?" He was being pulled over near Area 51 by state police. He pulled over and watched them in the rear view mirror. One cop had a night stick and was slapping it into his hand. The other one had his gun drawn. "Okay Green get out of the vehicle and assume the position." Jake did as they told him to do. "Officer what did I do?" "Damn, that is pathetic you know it Frank?" "Yea, he's a dumb fuck." "Hey Cap." "What are we going to do with this piece of shit?" "I know Frank!" "We'll bring him to that Air Force facility where they experiment on aliens." "Hell, they can find out what the fuck is wrong with him." "Sir, why am I being detained?" Jake said in a polite voice. "Did you hear something Frank?" "Yea I think I heard him pissing his pants." "He may have shit himself too." They laughed hysterically. "Look, numb nuts just stand there and shut the fuck up." Frank told Jake. "You are one sorry son of a bitch asshole." Cap said. "I'll have to wake you up with this night stick." He hit Jake across his back and head several times. "Now any more fucking questions?" "I didn't think so." Frank punched him in the nose and he heard a Pop!" "I think I broke his nose." He said. "Ah shit look at all that blood." "Quit bleeding all over my highway shit for brains." Frank told Jake. "You know I think he's a druggie." Cap said. "Yea we better strip search him." Frank said. "I'm not touching him!" Cap said laughing. "Well, pecker head what the fuck are you carrying drugs in your hippie van for?" Cap asked Jake. Jake refused to answer and said, "I want to speak to a lawyer." "You wanna what!?" Frank asked. The cops laughed hysterically. "Do you see any asshole lawyers out here in the desert

shit for brains?" "Smartin the fuck up Hippie."
Cap said. Frank placed a bag of marijuana in Jake's
shirt pocket and spilled some on the seat of the
van. Then he spilled some cocaine in the glove
compartment."Lookie here Cap." "I found his pot
stash." "Oh man I found his coke too." "Collect the
evidence and we'll bring him in for questioning."
Cap told Frank. "Looks like your going to jail for
a long time Green." "It'll keep your spying ass
out of trouble." "The Air Force will love this."
Frank yelled to Cap. "That's right hippie we're
just following orders." "It's nothing personnel."
Cap said as he smashed Jake with his night stick.
"Ouch, that hurt you bastard!" Jake said. "Well
ain't that too fucking bad." "Now fuck face, take
your shitty cloths off." "We may have to beat a
confession out of him Cap." Jake pretended to start
taking his cloths off and ran into the desert and
tried to escape. The cops radioed headquarters for
a K9 unit. As he was running like hell he fell into
a pit with concrete walls. There was a trap door
which he forced open. It led to an underground
tunnel. "I don't know where I am but, it's better
then up there." He told himself. There was a maze
of tunnels and portals leading in all directions.
He looked for a set of stairs or elevator. Finally
he found some stairs and took them. As he ran
down them he heard voices. "Hey, Bob why are we
always the ones to examine this alien shit?" "We're
just lucky." "This is some nasty smelling stuff."
"When did this one crash?" "The stealth jets shot
a UFO down yesterday and they removed these

bodies." "Well, I've got to take a shit and need a break." The workmen left and Jake saw the alien bodies. Since he didn't have a camera he took some of the clothing and a tissue sample from an alien's body. Then he got right out of there. He made his way to the surface and was in the middle of Area 51. "I better go back through the tunnels." He finally located his van and drove off. The cops had left and it was like nothing had ever happened.

When he found a motel he cleaned up and then checked out right away. "I'll take my evidence to the one place I know will play it." "I'll go to the underground press." "They're not afraid of anything." The Georgia Straight in Canada and that Rag paper in Kansas were underground papers Jake knew about from his business world days. The Underground Press in Canada and the International Times in England were also options. "There are tons of these "alternative papers" around the world." Jake mused. Jake decided to head for Canada to Manitoba and Vancouver. The Underground Press in Manitoba would be his first stop. Then he'd head for Vancouver and the Georgia Straight. "I'll see what Suzie's up to and pack all my evidence." Jake had a scheme all worked out. "Once the underground press starts printing my evidence the American Press will pay me big bucks for it." "Now, that's being a capitalist!" "How to make a buck in America!"

Suzie had gone home and was on call for an actress job in San Francisco. She was also a stripper and "dancer." Jake called around and couldn't locate her, so he drove to Fairfield where she had a apartment. After several days of asking around he tried one last thing. "I'll check the strip joints and see if she's "dancing". Sure enough, he found her in a rather seedy joint near Travis AFB. As he sat watching her perform he drank a $5.00 beer and smiled at her. Finally she saw him and sat down at his table. "Buy me a drink cowboy?" "Sure honey anything you want." As they drank their rather expensive beers she said, "look Jake I'm not going on any more wild goose chases." "I've got to work." "Okay honey, but hear me out cause I'm gona make lots of bucks." "I'm selling my evidence to the media and hell you took some of the pictures and deserve some of the profits." "That's alright Jake, but no thanks." "Bring some other babe with you." "I'm saving up for a new bike." "I'm buying you a Harley." Jake promised her. "You are my kind of woman." "And what does that mean?" "You need a companion and sex toy right?" Jake noticed a tear in her eyes and started feeling guilty and like a real low life. "I guess I have been neglecting you for this project." "Jake your crazy and I love you, but where are we?" "Nowhere, that's where!" She yelled. "Look honey I'll do anything you want and all you have to do is call me." He got up to leave and she said,"come by my place later and we'll see." "Okay!!" She had to dance and Jake left. "She's too beautiful for that crap and I'll show her a better life." "I've got to collect on an old debt before we leave for Canada." Jake had been partners in a small business with a dude in San Fran and was planning to sell his half. They had a whole sale organic food warehouse on the docks and made big bucks." He drove into the city and found his partner at the local watering hole on Market street near the old Fillmore West. Jake got a check for his shares and headed back to see Suzie. Suzie was just getting home when he knocked at the door. "Hey baby are you ready to leave?" "Right now Jake?" "Hell yes we're heading for Canada." "To where?" "Why Canada?" "It's colder then the North Pole up there!" "Bring your long johns and mukluks." Jake told her.

The van was loaded up and ready to go. They decided to take I-80 East to I-15 North in Salt Lake City, to I-90 East to I-94 East to I-29 North. From there it was a straight to Manitoba. It was August and the weather was fine. After camping in the Rockies for three nights they stayed in Emerson, Canada, a quiet town, mostly mining and lumber camps. They found a unique little chalet for rent and stayed for a couple nights. Between the Northern Lights and the Fall foliage they were able to enjoy cooking over an open fire. "This moose steak is damn tasty." Suzie said while chomping on a rib. "Yea, but I love the bear pudding." Jake said. "You know what I heard?" "That game suppers of wild animals are a healthy dinner and you don't get tired after eating." "Well, Jake you are how old now?" "You look about 60!" "Yea, there's a lot of mileage on these feet and my brain is riddled with drugs from my younger party days!" "That why you get so damned tired!" She told her burned out boyfriend Jake Green.

The next morning they headed out for Snow Lake, Manitoba and the Underground Press. But, not before an alarm woke them up. It was a mine cave in. The entire town was up and in a frenzy. "Come on Jake let's cover the story." When they arrived with their camera and tape recorder the town emergency squad was setting up shop. Jake took pictures and Suzie interviewed people. After about two hours the elevator doors from the mine opened and out came the trapped miners. A huge applause went up and everybody went into the local bar. The trapped miners were there and Suzie spoke with them while Jake filmed it. "Sir what is your name?" Suzie asked. "What's that ya say thar honey?" "What is your name?" "Ma name?" "Oh Yea I thank it's, it's Jim Hackin-nuts." "Sir, what was it like down there?" "It was, was a, a sort touch and go at first and then we was drinkin some booze." "Yes sir, we was happy as a pig in a poke!" Another miner said. "Damn, they smell like a pig in shit!" Jake said to himself. "Well, they got some Canadian Whiskey down thar ta us and we done drank it." "Mr. Hackin-nuts, you mean you all got drunk?" Suzie asked. "No, no, not exactly I wouldn't say thart honey not rale, rale drunk." "We might a got a little bit drunk tho cause we drank so much!" "Ha, Ha, Ha!" "But, it was smooth as silk." "That Canadian Club Whiskey is real sippin whiskey." ""Yes sir it tis." "We done drunk and finished off bout six bottles er so and then them rescue men done broke in and off we come ta hare there honey pie." The miner held up a bottle of Canadian Club and said, "thanks fur the booze." "You see honey Canadian Club, thar gona give us a life time supply of them's best whiskey." "It saved our dirty asses." "Now I'm getting drunk ever day from naw on!" Jim Hackin-nuts said smiling with no teeth. "His breath smells like a combination of dog shit and cheap booze." Jake said to Suzie. "I freaking know that Jake!" She yelled. "Have you ever seen a more pathetic and senile out coot?" "No way hero!" Suzie said. Another miner said, "hey honey come over here!" She sat next to him and listened to his story. All the miners loved Suzie and gave her in depth coverage of the cave in. "The headline will read, "Miners saved by Canadian Club Whiskey." Jake yelled to Suzie. The next day they sold the story to CNN for $1000. "Jake you've really got something here." Suzie said while kissing him."Yea, but I won't ever forget that Hackin-nuts creep." "Damn he smelled like the bottom of a bird cage!"

They arrived late that day at the Underground Press and it was closed. A note on the door said, "call me at home, MJ". Finally they found the editor's home and met with him. "MJ" was not real thrilled about the UFO story. But, he'd print it anyway. He figured he'd get a lot of grief from people for printing a story about a crashed UFO that USAF jets supposedly shot down! The paper went out over the world wide web and Jake was happy about that. They found an Inn and checked in. Once in their room Suzie ran into the bathroom and started a hot bath. "Honey, I'll get the booze and you soak." "Okay lover." Jake poured drinks for them both and brought Suzie hers. As he sank into the couch he felt really good for the first time in years. He wasn't getting paid yet for the UFO story, but it just felt right. "Looks like I found myself as a reporter." He yelled to Suzie.

"What next Jake?" Suzie looked at him with kind, but questioning eyes. "The other Canadian underground paper." "It's in Vancouver." "No way Jake!" "Let's wait and see if we get any offers from regular media outlets." "Okay, but first we go to Kansas and that rag under ground paper." "It's straight down through Canada and the U.S. from here baby!"

After giving their story to that rag they went home. Back at Suzie's pad they passed out in bed exhausted." Jake woke up and put on CNN. There were pictures of a crashed UFO and Air Force jets. The CNN reporter, Dan Miller, kept saying the same thing over and over. "Jake and Suzie Green took these pictures near an Air Force base one month age." "It is unbelievable, but real the reporter said!" "Suzie get up!" "What the hell Jake." "No, baby come here we're on CNN." As they watched, the pictures of the jets shooting the UFOs down flashed across the screen. "Jake's voice could be heard saying, "there it goes down in flames." "I'm in my van now and chasing it." Pictures of the wreck and the choppers filled the CNN screen. "Thank God they think you're name is Suzie Green or they'd be here now." "Yea, now let's get the hell out of here!" She screamed. All their things were still in the van and they headed East to Island Pond, Vermont. Suzie knew some church people there they could hide out with. They picked up the van in Needles and got rid of the "FBI" car. The van was now white with red trim.

Driving clear across the U.S. In a VW Van is not easy when you're trying to hide from the law and the military. So, they camped out in the daytime and drove at night. They arrived in Island Pond five days later. Island Pond is a quiet little Northern Vermont town. Tucked away near the Canadian border it was perfect for Jake and Suzie. The Church put them up and hid them out from the cops.

"How long are we staying here Jake?" "Until we figure out if they're after us." "In the meantime we cover stories and send in the copy for pay." "Jake, there's no news here." "It's dead." "True and we may travel around looking for news." "We can always call CNN for a story." "Okay Jake I'm tired and going to bed." Jake stayed up thinking about ways to get stories. Anyway, Jake had other plans. He knew some musicians in Burlington who wanted to play out in bars. He'd get a band going and start playing out while Suzie did her dancing, acting thing. Now that they felt safe from the cops it was time to get paying jobs. Suzie quickly became all the rave in Burlington, a college town. She was booked into several night spots and on call as an actress in the Burlington Playhouse.

Jake and his band were playing out on weekends and one night an agent from a recording company heard them. Jake got a contract to record his new song, "Tombstone Blues." It would appear with some other local bands on a CD. Meanwhile, Suzie was looking so good that Playboy offered her a photo spread in the November edition. "Look, Jake I've got to take this job." "I need the money and the my name up in lights." Suzie told him at the bar she danced in. "Okay babe, but remember I warned you about the vampires out there." "I think you're jealous Jake!" "No way babe, just concerned for your safety." "Yea, sure!" "I have to be at the Playboy Mansion in LA tomorrow lover." Jake drove her to the airport for her flight to LA. He wished her well and told her to hurry back. As he drove off alone he kept singing an old Neil Young song. "I think I'd like to go back home and take it easy. Tired of all this day to day running around. Everybody knows this is nowhere."

Chapter 4:

Honky Tonk Woman

"What the hell I might as well party with friends in B Town." Jake told himself. He headed over to Burlington for a little partying. His party buddy there was Bill Harty, ("Billy Bicardi") and his brother Hugh Harty, ("Huge Party"). They lived with some babes near the lake and were always ready for some action. In Burlington that amounts to smoking pot and boozing it up. There are lots of night clubs that the college kids frequent. Mostly rock bands are jamming and people are having fun. As he arrived at the friends home he saw three beautiful babes going inside. He knocked on the door, "hey Billy, Hugh what's up?" "Come on in whoever you are." A voice yelled. It was Billy and he looked wasted. "Billy you look all partied out." Jake said. "Ahh, you could say that." "Is that you Jake?" "Smoke this Billy." Jake handed him a huge joint. "That's just what the doctor ordered." Billy said as he took a pull. After they got totally wasted they went out to some bars. At the "B Town Copacabana Club" on Church street, "Billy Bicardi" and "Huge Party" both lived up to their names. Within two hours they were both dancing on the bar naked with UVM Coeds. This went on for what seemed hours and Jake finally had enough and split.

Now that Suzie was gone Jake felt very different. He didn't feel like playing guitar or writing. Then one night the drummer quit the band right in the middle of "already gone", by the "Eagles." The guy said he'd had enough and was leaving for Australia. A new UFO sighting was reported in the underground press. Jake called his friend at the press and found out it was seen at Mackenzie Bay, in the Yukon Territory. "What the hell am I doing in Burlington, Vermont?" "Color me gone baby!" "I'll pack up, say goodbye to the church folks and head out." "First I'll park the van in Island Pond then rent an FBI Ford for the trip." "The Van has a lousy heater and I want a new car for this trip." It's a long haul." I'll take I-80 to Chicago, I-94 to Fargo, I-29 to Winnipeg, Can. Route 16 to Terrace, Can. Route 37 to Can. Route 1 to Whitehorse and then Can. Route 2 to Dawson." He got the van stored and said goodbye to the church folks. "I'm on my way, color me gone baby."

As he drove along I-80 he kept thinking about how Suzie would be nude in Playboy. "She'll be dancing her way across the damn country." "She will no doubt be nude worldwide on the net." "Hey wait a minute." "That's it!" "If she uses the name Suzie Green she can become the "UFO Playboy Bunny!" "She could be the "UFO Queen" or the "UFO Sex Goddess." "What more can I ask for." "It's free advertising!" "I'm really pressing this and I have got to concentrate on my driving." He had left Vermont at 5am and was not tired. "I think I'll check out Wright Paterson Field for UFOs." He drove over to the Air Force Base located near Dayton,Ohio. He looked for Hanger 18 and snooped around the huge base.. Jake got a visitors pass and had breakfast in the chow hall. Nobody was talking much and he decided to do some investigating. "Finally after four hours of walking all over the base I asked some airmen where the damned Hanger 18 was." "They were very friendly and helpful and told me that hanger 18 was just a myth." Jake being stubborn and persistent continued to look. "This is a huge facility and they could be hiding UFO debris almost anywhere." Jake told himself. Since he could not find any sign of a UFO or Hanger 18 he took a new approach to the problem. "I'll dress up in the FBI outfit and fake it." He told himself with an evil grin on his wolf man looking face. Once he got all changed into the FBI cloths he started acting all official and walked right into headquarters. "Airman!" He said to the sergeant on duty. "Yes sir how can I help you?" "You can help me sergeant by directing me to the OD!" Jake said as he flashed his fake FBI I.D. card."Yes sir right away sir." "Major Beam, the FBI is here to see you sir." "Send him in sergeant." "Yes sir." "Go ahead in sir." Jake walked into the Major's office like he owned the place. "Major I need immediate access to Hanger 18 and the latest recovered UFO debris." Jake demanded as he flashed his fake ID.

"Alright, but please show me your authorization credentials." "Look Major this is a matter of national security and you need to move it!" "Now direct me to the Hanger 18 at once!" "I'm sorry sir But....." "Give me the damn phone Major I'm calling the president." "This is his orders you are flagrantly disobeying!" "I'll have your ass and your commission over this!" "Sergeant call base security at once." The Major said ordering his First Sergeant into action. "Yes sir." The Major told Jake to sit down and shut up. "Who are you really mister?" "Your ass is mine!" The Major said with a shit eating grin on his face. Jake figured his little charade was over and bolted. As he ran out of the Major's office alarms started going off. "I'll never make it out of here alive." He yelled to himself. Once at the main gate he acted official and made it out of the base. "Well, I guess the Air Force isn't using Hanger 18 anymore." "At least not right out in the open!" Jake had discovered that his new career as a journalist can be tricky and frustrating and even dangerous. As he drove off he noticed three SR-71 Blackbirds taking off in formation. The huge monsters were firing their continuous bleed afterburning turbines and burning up the sky above Wright Paterson AFB. "Tower this is Cap K on vector Romeo, Charlie, Delta One Zero climbing out to Eight Zero at Zulu time." "That's a wilco Cap K." "Cap K and flight out." "Damn those babies are scary." "Maybe I just saw the real UFOs!" Jake said staring into the space that the mighty Blackbirds once possessed. "The fastest jet aircraft that has even flown is a real UFO right here on Earth!"

Back on the road Jake was pushing it too hard. "I'm too damned pumped up to be tired." "I'm going straight through to Winnipeg damn it!" "When I get there I'll see my friends at the Underground Press and find out more about this new UFO sighting." He was hitting 90 mph on the interstate and it was clear sailing. He had a V8 in the "FBI Ford" and it really hauled ass. "These damn fool FBI agents don't fool around!" "They haul ass and catch the bad guys." "If I get pulled over I'll tell the cops I'm an agent on vacation or something." "They'll have a good laugh." Jake was getting a little loopy and goofy from driving. "I can see it all now," and he drifted off and imagined the cops pulling him over... "Sir, license and registration please." "Yes, sir officer." "Sir, did you know I clocked you a 100mph!" "Ah, well officer I'm an agent on vacation." "You're a what?!" "Hey Bob did hear what he said?" The first cop said to his partner. "Yea sarge I heard it and wonder what he's smoking." "You're a fucking agent?" "From where the planet Mars?" "Get the fuck out of the car secret agent man!" "Now assume the position shit head." "Hey Bob is Larry on duty tonight at the barracks?" "Yea sarge and I know he'll want to question this piece of shit." "I think after we shock him with the taser and throw him in the cell he'll start to cooperate." "Yea, after he rots in there for a couple years he'll come around!" They were cracking up and acting like cops on drugs. "I think he just pissed his pants sarge." "No fucking way." "Let him go I don't want my brand new cop car, Super Ford Interceptor Special all pissed on." "Okay shit face you can go now." "Have a nice day shit for brains!" "Ha, Ha, Ha!"

Jake snapped out of it as he almost drove off the road. "I better slow the hell down." "I guess the old FBI routine won't work for shit." "I've got white line fever again." "It's all getting kind of blurry." "I had better get the hell off of the highway." He pulled over at a rest stop and passed out in the car. When he woke up it was 9am and the sun was shinning in his eyes. "Holy shit!" "I better go." He drove right on down the pike. "Going down the road feeling bad." "Yea going down the road feeling bad." "I just lost the best friend I ever had." Jake sang the old Greatful Dead song.

After about forty more Dead songs and eight cups of coffee he pulled into Winnipeg at 11pm and found a Holiday Inn. "Shit, I'm not tired and need a drink." He went down on the strip and found a cowboy bar. It was Friday night and the place was rocking. Everybody looked like a cross between Willy Nelson and Johnny Cash. The juke box was blaring. "Here I am at Folsom prison...." "I've been everywhere yea, I been everywhere..." The "Coyote Club" bar was Winnipeg's version of a Texas Country and Western bar on a Saturday night. "Shit it's got all the right stuff, but it looks all wrong! Jake said shaking his foggy head. " It's the place to go for Canadian Cowboys on the make." "These "Cowboys" are in heat for those strange looking Canadian Cowgirls over there." Jake said to himself as he looked at the group of girls at the bar. They had cowgirl shirts, boots, and shorts on." "Cowgirls don't wear shorts unless their the Dallas Cowboys Cheerleaders." "Shit, that's it they're copying the Dallas Cowboys Cheerleaders!" "The freaking cowboys here are copying Clint Eastwood or Roy Rogers!" He said laughing.

There certainly was a strange atmosphere in these Canadian cowboy bars. It was like they didn't quite know how to act as real cowboys, in say Texas. Jake bellied up to the bar and ordered Jim Beam on the rocks. "What you drinking that piss for boy." "This here is Canada and we all drink Canadian whiskey." The strange looking Canadian cowboy was starting to piss Jake off. "Okay, then let's see if any thing you buy can compare with Jim Beam." Jake said. "That's simple there boy." The redneck said. "Give me two Canadian Clubs Charlie." The redneck Canadian Cowboy ordered the drinks. They drank them down and Jake said, "now taste some real bourbon whiskey." "This is from real whiskey making country in Kentucky, America." They chugged them down and the redneck said, "not to bad pal." "Guess you're right." This went on for awhile and Jake was getting drunk. He decided to try his luck with the cowgirls. "Hi cowgirl can I buy you and your cowgirl friends a drink?" He said as he walked up to them. They all started laughing and one of them said, "you American?" "Yea honey I am." "Are you from Dallas?" She asked. "Yea I am and I'm a cattle rancher." They all laughed again. Jake ordered them all tequila. "This here is what we all drink down in Texas." "Best place on Earth." Jake said acting like a cowboy. Three Canadian Cowboys came up to the bar and asked the cowgirls to dance. "Hey buddy these here are our girls now beat it!" The biggest one said to Jake. "Sure pal I was just leaving." "They're all yours!" "These fool cowboys don't even have Colt 45's strapped to their leg." "They must be fake!"

Since he was getting drunk he figured he'd better head back to his room. As he slept while passed out on his bed the TV set was playing a re-run of the "Good, the Bad and the Ugly." Clint Eastwood just blew away Lee Van Cleef and found the gold in the graveyard. As Clint rode away his ex partner, Eli Wallach's voice rang out, " blondie you bastard, your mother should rot in hell...." Then a special news announcement came on. "This is Dan Miller at CNN headquarters and I am reporting the sighting of another UFO in Canada." Jake was snoring now and unaware of the news he had wanted to hear.

The next day he left early and planned to drive straight through to Whitehorse. "The Yukon is where I really want to be." "These Americanized Canadians are fake." He put the "FBI" car on the highway and headed North at 100mph! Through towns and villages and the country side he had only one thing on his mind. "Was this another Air Force fake UFO?" "I will find out damn it!" "Herschel Island?" "Sounds like Herschel Walker the football player." "The strip joints in Winnipeg will be a far cry from where I'm going." His mind was full of thoughts and he couldn't focus on his driving. "That sirloin steak I had back in Winnipeg may be the last real food I'll get for a long time." There were a few trucks on the road and he spaced out during periods of just black pavement and white lines. "White line fever." "That's what I've got again damn it all." "I'll have to make a pit stop at a truck stop." "Why Mackenzie Bay?" He asked himself while in a white line fever fog. "What the hell is up there worth knowing about for aliens." "Maybe they were off course or came out of warp speed there." "It's very near to Alaska and the U.S." "That means it's either an Air Force experimental spacecraft, or a real UFO spying on the Air Force again." He told himself again. "This time I've got to get at the truth!"

"MacKenzie Bay, named after Captain Mackenzie of the ship Discovery in 1931." "Tuktoyakuk is near by." He said to himself. "The Eskimo's there are friendly and had a early warning radar site in the fifties and sixties and beyond." "It was part of the Air Force "Dew Line", an early warning system ." "We dropped the big one on Japan and the beginning of the end was in sight!" Jake told himself shaking his dizzy head. "America used nuclear weapons on Japan and that's how it all got started." "That was a Cold War thing." "Everybody in the U.S. was worried about Russia and a nuclear attack." "So, we built more and more nuclear missiles so we'd have more then Russia." "The freaking Arms Race was on!" "America and

Russia in an insane contest to see who could build the most nuclear weapons!" "We created enough of them to blow the world up a hundred times!" "But, we still kept building more!" "This Dew Line was suppose to give us enough advance warning to prepare for a nuclear attack from the Russians." "Of course, how the hell do you prepare for a nuclear attack?" "Hell, they just wanted to fire their nukes at Russia!" "Retaliation!" Jake told himself. "I think the aliens knew all about this shit and that's why there were so many UFO sightings back then." "The damned aliens were spying on us and Russia!" "We didn't like that very much and now we're blasting them out of the sky." "If we could we'd bomb them back into the Stone Age like in Vietnam." "The U.S, military don't like no aliens in flying saucers telling them what to do, damn it all to hell!!" "That's our redneck American Military for you!" Jake told himself in a disgusted voice.

"My mind is wandering again." He told himself as he drank another cup of coffee. "Let's see." "Herschel Island was settled by the Hudson Bay Co. and is an Eskimo hunting village." "Some oil and gas exploration has been there too." "But, basically they are both dead areas and of no interest to aliens." "But, it's isolated and a good place for Air Force testing of new space craft reverse engineered from downed alien space craft." Jake was really confused and tired now. He was starting to realize just how convoluted and complicated the entire UFO cover up process was. What started out as a simple plan by the Air Force to confuse the American Public after the Roswell UFO Crash of 1947, had gotten completely out of control. The Air Force had assigned several new officers to take control of the cover up project. No one seemed to be able to handle the job. That's why it became so complicated, fragmented and unbelievable.

Jake knew the area and history, but it didn't answer any of his questions. "If it was the Air Force how the hell did they re-assemble the alien UFO?" Jake was really more confused then ever. "I can't stand being lost and confused!" "Here I am on the road to the Yukon Territory and for what?" "Damn I'm mixed up." He realized the fun was gone. Suzie made him happy and they really hit it off. "The trip is getting to me and I'm getting drunk tonight." It was about another three thousand miles to Whitehorse and Jake needed rest. Finally, he stopped at Battleford to get drunk. He hit several "cowboy" bars and staggered around the town. There were crazy things happening. "The people here all seem like robots." He slurred the words to himself. "No one will even look at me." "Maybe they're all aliens!" He saw a group of people and yelled at them. "Hey you over there." "Are you freaking aliens?" "They're ignoring me again damn it." "Hey!" "What the hell is your special problem?" "Don't freaking tell me assholes!" "Screw them and the white horse they rode in on." "Maybe I'll go to Whitehorse." "Did you hear that." "Shit on you and your town!" He crawled back to his room at the Best Western and passed out.

The next day Jake was hung over bad. "Should I try a little bit of the dog that bit me?" "No." "I've got to drive." "Maybe I better sleep it off." He passed out until 5pm. After a cold shower he felt better and was determined to get to Whitehorse. In Saskatoon he spotted a Holiday Inn and stayed for the night. It was like being in America, except the food tasted like army food or some other frozen, packaged food. He went to the Elk Club Disco and listened to the band play. Neil Young came out and did a set with his band Crazy Horse. "Neil said, "I'm from Canada and lived in LA for awhile as an illegal alien." "This song is dedicated to all aliens, legal and illegal." Jake asked himself if illegal aliens were the real aliens. "That's the only aliens I've ever met." He told himself. After the set Jake took off. The next morning he got an early start. He kept plugging away and thought to himself, "I stayed in a Holiday Inn Express and I can solve the biggest freaking riddle of our time." "There are no UFOs." "The Air Force was right." "Now I can go home." "That dream I had last night at the Express was bad news." "Suzie was all naked at the Playboy Mansion and stripping for all those horny men." "She was right," "I am a jealous idiot."

Chapter 5:

The Naked Truth

Suzie woke up to a loud booming sound outside her window at the mansion. It was a jet chopper and two men dressed in black were coming into her room. "Miss, we need to fly you to FBI Headquarters in LA." They were playboy security and meant business. "I have my photo shoot today." "Sorry miss we have our orders." "From whom?" "From FBI." "Oh alright mind if I get dressed!" "Please hurry Miss." As they led "Mrs. Green" from her room she wondered what the hell this was all about. They landed in the desert near some buildings. "This isn't LA!" She exclaimed. "Sorry miss we have our orders." "What do they want with me?" "Sorry miss we don't know." "The last time we flew someone here they were never seen or heard from again." Now she was really scared. She began shaking and mumbling a prayer. They took her to large room with one light on and water running onto a wooden board. Two men dressed in black stood staring at her and there was total silence. "Why am I here?" They had blank expressions on their faces and refused to speak. She tried to leave and was locked in. "What the hell do you perverts want with me?" "Answer me you dirty bastards!" She went over and kicked one of them on the balls. "He won't even move when kicked in the balls!" She yelled. "Maybe they don't have any balls!" "I think they're robots!" She gave up and tried to break out. "There is no way out of here!" Finally she fell asleep and when she woke up she was naked and tied to the board. Water was running into her mouth as she was tilted back. She began choking as though drowning. "I can't breath you perverts!" "You sick bastards like torturing women?" "May you all rot in hell!" She passed out and woke up again with the same torture. This went on for what seemed days and she was about to expire when the water finally stopped. A loud piercing voice yelled, "now talk!" "Tell us about the UFO." "What UFO!" She yelled. The voice kept repeating the same words over and over. Then the water started again. Finally she yelled, "okay I was with a friend who saw a UFO crash and we followed it around." "Okay?" Now the water was trickling and she was being shocked. "Ahh!, you bastards!" "I'll kill you every one of you pricks!" "We'll track you all down and murder you all one by one in a slow, painful death!" She yelled at them. They kept shocking her until she passed out. When she woke up this time she was lying in the desert with her cloths on. "I have no idea where I am." She had dried blood on her face and her head and side hurt. "I remember falling on to the concrete floor and passing out." "Now what do I do?"

Jake was driving into Moose Jaw and realized he was starved. He had been day dreaming for hours about Suzie and it was already 6pm. He had been going 100mph all day and had made good time. He checked into the "Hunter's Haven" and went out to eat. At the "Baby Moose Grill" he ordered ale and steak. The moose steak was really tender and the french fries were great. He later spoke with some hunters. "Hey there mister you drinking alone?" "Yea." "Well, join us for a shot and a beer." Big Charlie said. "Listen, you guys from here?" "No not really." "What's your name?" Jake asked. "I'm Little John Swartz and I'm a hunter and trapper, of people sometimes." He said laughing. "And I'm Big Charlie Gingo and I'm a trapper too." "No one is from here year round that is." "This is a hunter's town." "Those french fries were out of this world." Jake said. "They should be they were made from tip top whale blubber." "No way!" Jake said almost puking. "Oh yea, they are great." Charlie said with a stupid look on his face. "We just shot the moose you ate this morning." "I gutted it up myself." "Little John Swartz said as he drooled on his shirt. Jake was starting to get a little sick to his stomach. "We had Elk yesterday." "The damned thing ran through a window and killed himself." Big Charlie said while spitting a chew of tobacco on the floor. "We gutted up right on the spot." Big Charlie said with his toothless mouth." Little John said, "hell we stay here all Summer and Fall." "You wanna go out with us huntin in the morn?" "I really can't." Jake said. "Listen, have you guys heard about anything strange happening around here?" Jake asked. " No, I can't say we have." Little John said. "Jake said, " you know, the UFO reports?" "You mean the Air Force jets up at Mackenzie Bay?" "You guys know about it?" "There ain't no UFOs mister." "We think it's a crock of shit." "Them is Air Force planes." Big Charlie said as he cut a huge, rotten smelling fart. Jake finished his Moose Head Ale, Moose steak and Moose pie and left the Baby Moose Grill."Damn, those guys were the biggest cretins I've ever met!"

An old timer was cleaning the lobby at the Haven and Jake asked him about the UFO. "Mister tell me about the flying saucer?" "What's dat yas say thar young fella?" "What's your name sir?" "What's it to ya?" "I'm a reporter." "Yar a what?" "I am a CNN reporter." "Oh ya." "Well I'll tell ya ma name is Tony Graziano and I'm from Italy." Jake could smell him from ten feet away. "He smells like a combination of the worst body order in the world and cow shit!" Jake mumbled to himself. "Doesn't anybody in this town take a bath!" He asked himself. "Mr. Graziano did you see the UFO?" "Ya mean the drunkin elk?" "Got no time ta talk naw." "I seen that afor one time." "I did, I did see it." "I ain't lyin to yas nope." "I thank da elk was drunk." "Everyting and body is always drunk hare." "Why ya askin?" "I'm a reporter." Jake said. "Your a what!?" "Well I'll be." "I seen em too." "You saw what?" Jake asked. "I seen thum aliens." "Thum is flying around hare all da time." "You know bout em?" He said as he drank some cheap port wine. "He appears to be drunk or high on something." Jake said to himself. "Wha, wha da yas wants ta naw fur?" He said slurring his words. "What's that smell!" Jake said to himself as he put some more distance between them. "Ya seen em too?" "Yea I think so." Jake said. "Well good luck ta ya naw." Jake took off in a hurry and went to bed.

Suzie got a ride to Bakersfield and located some old friends. She called the church folks in Island Pond and they told her to stay put and Jake would call her. Finally, three days later Jake called about Suzie at the Playboy club and was told she had checked out in a hurry. He got concerned and called the church folks who told him where she was. He located her and made arrangements for her to fly to Prince George and he would meet her at the airport. As he waited for the Air Canada flight from LA he realized how bad he had it for Suzie. The plane made a perfect landing right on time. He spotted her and let out a cowboy yell,"yahoo"and "yippee kiyee." She looked so perfect with her long blond hair and perfect body. "Come here baby I've been missing you." Jake said in a romantic voice. "Oh god Jake I'm so glad to see you." Jake hauled off and kissed her for so long it took her breath away. "Come on baby I've got a room at the "Canadian Lodge." "It's all stocked up with booze and food." "We won't have to go anywhere for a few days." "Suzie started crying and Jake held her tight and took her to his room.

By the time Jake and Suzie came up for air it was three days later. After she told him about the Air Force torture he promised her it would never happen again. "I know how to beat these bastards." Jake told her. "I've got something on them now and I will contact my lawyer right away." Jake called his LA lawyer, Ben Kilmartin and put him to work on the case. "Suzie, we'll get the bastards!" "You know Jake, I will never strip for anyone except you ever again." "That's my girl baby." Jake and Suzie had found each other. Now Jake had to find himself.

"How's your lawyer going to prove anything?" Suzie asked him. "It won't be easy and it never is." "I will take appropriate action   myself to pay them back for what they did to you." Jake told her. They hit the road early and made good time to Hazelton and route 37 North. "Next stop Whitehorse baby."

Driving into Whitehorse in the Yukon Territory was a trip Jake and Suzie will never forget. "Jake I think of all the old miners and prospectors that came here in 1898 during the Klondike Gold Rush." "Yea baby and you can bet they suffered for every ounce of gold they took out." "They had to walk every foot up to the gold fields on the Klondike." "No snow mobiles or planes, just mushers." Jake said. "There's a nice looking place to stay." Suzie said. "The Chilkoot Trail Inn" was all lit up like a Christmas tree. "Okay baby let's do it." After they checked in they went to the "Roadhouse Inn" for dinner. "I'll take the caribou stew and the moose pie". Jake said and " I'll take the elk ribs and fries with moose salad". Suzie said. They wolfed down their meal and had Yukon Jack whiskey to wash it down. "That was great and I'm stuffed." Suzie said. "Let's hit the sack." Jake said.

The next day they toured the town. Actually it surprised them how big a town it was. There were three movie houses, four bowling alleys, three drug stores, two hardware stores and 110 bars! "Let's go in there." Jake said. "Ziggy's Rock Shop" was the only music store in town. It was plastered with Greatful Dead posters and Neil Young pictures. A huge water pipe was sitting on a round table in the middle of the shop. "Want a hit?" The owner said to Suzie. "It's illegal." She said. Ziggy started laughing his fool head off. "No it ain't my dear girl." He went over and took a great big pull and exhaled a fog of pot smoke into the air. Jake took a hit and then Suzie. "Got any stones albums?" Jake asked. "Do Zebra's have stripes?" Ziggy replied. "I want the live one with "Honky Tonk woman." "Alright!" Jake grabbed the album. Ziggy was a ex hippie from the San Francisco Hippie days and had been in Whitehorse for 20 years. "I'll take this "Happy Trails" album too." Jake said. "Quicksilver Messenger Service a San Fran Band." Ziggy said. "I seen em once at the Fillmore." "No sir, I ain't never had a problem with smokin pot here." "Whitehorse is okay and the cops would rather have pot heads then drunks." "I grow it in a green house." "Hydroponics." "So, what about the UFO?" Suzie asked. "The UFO went down at

Mackenzie Bay bout four or five hundred miles North." Ziggy said. "The Air Force flies them over here all the time and we don't even think a thing about it." "Let's get stoned man." Ziggy said. "It's nice to see some real Americans up here."

After they left Ziggy's they went into the Sourdough Cafe. An old timer waited on them. "What will you have there pilgrims?" "We'll take coffee and eggs." "Okay there pilgrim." "Well, what you two doing up hare in God's Country?" "The UFO, I'm a reporter." "Well I declare." "I ain't never in all my born days seen a reporter like her." "Well I am and I would like to take your picture." Suzie said. "Well I just don't know bout that." The sourdough said. "What is your name sir?" Suzie asked. "Ma name is Bill Young and I'm waitin on ya." "I spose I'll be on CNN?" He asked "Yep, maybe." She replied. Suzie took the picture and Jake recorded him on audio. "About the UFO Mr. Young?" "Looky hare thare honey pie I ani't seein too good these hare days and I caint member much." "His breath smells like Buffalo shit and his teeth are all rotten." Jake said to himself. "Don't they have any freaking dentists up here?" Jake asked himself laughing. "So you didn't see anything?" Suzie asked. "I doesn't even member and I told yas so." "I did say I might have see a flyin saucer thang awhile back when." Mr. Bill Young took a drink of some cheap rot gut whiskey and then he cut a fart. "Damn that stinks!" Jake said out loud. "Sorry bout that thare mister." Bill said laughing. "I had beans fur dinnar." "Ha Ha."

"Good luck with that there flying saucer." "It's hidden real good they say." The old fart sourdough said. "Ain't seen it in bout a week now." "I don't know there pilgrim." "Might get yourself and the Mrs. arrested." He said. "I ain't takin no chances." "I don't mess around with no UFOs." "Rots a ruck, ha, ha, ha." They threw their food away and left. "I kind of lost my appetite." Jake said "No shit Sherlock!" Suzie said laughing.

"Let's go to the Reindeer Bar over there Jake." "Okay baby." It was apparent that booze was the main drug of choice in Whitehorse. Everybody was drunk by noon on weekends and by 3pm on weekdays. All Canadian bands were features on the juke box. Jake played, "Don't give me no hand me down World", by the Guess Who, Neil Young and Rory Gallagher, "a million miles away." "That's how I feel Jake." "A million miles away from here!" Suzie said. "It's all miners and tourists up here." Jake said. "What the hell did you expect?" "Rocket scientists?" Suzie asked.

Next they went to the police dept. Sgt, O'Neil was on duty and told them, "the crime rate is very low except with you reporters and tourists." "You see you people cause the problems." "Asking all your stupid questions and shit." "Why don't you take a long walk on a short peer." "We mean to keep it nice and peaceful so just clear out." "Any questions?" "One last question." Jake said. "What's the strangest thing that's happened here?" "Probably one of you reporters getting your damned head caved in down on Klondike street!"

"Now get going!" They decided to leave while they still could. "Jake we have nothing to call in do we?" "No baby." "Let's get going to Dawson."

CNN bought the story of Suzie's kidnapping and torture and that was all. Suzie's nude photos were on CNN the next day. Playboy had taken a few shots and sold them. The UFO story still wasn't happening. As they drove into Dawson it was starting to snow and they needed warmer cloths. They found a trapper's store and bought fur coats and hats. Dawson is an old time Gold Rush town in Northern Canada. There are still some merchants around and some miners. As they arrived Jake said, "let's stay at the "Downtown Hotel" and visit the "Klondike Sun" newspaper. The Royal Canadian Mounties had three battalions based in Dawson and they didn't believe in bothering people. "Keep an eye out for the Mounties." "They patrol around here." Jake said to Suzie. "It's a town out of touch with the world and there isn't much news to report." Suzie said. The room wasn't too bad considering it was Yukon Territory. "Jake there's no TV in this room." "There is a large tub for a hot bath and I'm in it now!" They needed a four wheel drive to get up to Mackenzie bay. When Jake went to rent the 4 wheel drive Land Rover he was told the last one was rented by CNN. "You mean they are already up there?" "Yes sir they left yesterday." "I have to get to Fort McPherson and to Inuvik." Jake said. "Sorry pal." Now Jake was pissed off. He called CNN and spoke to a reporter. "Mr. Miller what's going on!" "This is my story."

"Sorry Jake CNN bought it from you and we're all over it now." "But, seeing how I like you guys and want to get in on this I'll fly up there and meet you tomorrow." "We'll take a jet chopper up there and beat the CNN crew." "Okay man, but don't let me down." "I've got a surprise for you Jake." "See you tomorrow."

The next day Jake and Suzie laid out their plans and finally Mr. Miller arrived. "Is that Bill Wilson from Area 51 fame with them?" "He's a nuclear physicist!" Suzie said excitedly. "Damn I don't know." Jake said. Mr. Miller introduced himself and said, "I'd like you both to meet none other then Bill Wilson." "It's a pleasure to know you." Jake said. "Listen let's have dinner and get you guys a room." Suzie said. They checked in to the hotel and had dinner. Mr. Wilson was laughing his head off. "Finally, I will prove they really exist." Bill said grinning ear to ear. "It's been a long time coming." "I worked at Area 51 and at other secret, experimental bases." "Now we may finally prove that UFOs exist and that the Air Force and military have copied alien technology for years." "First we have to see what they have up there." Jake said. "Mr. Miller can you get clearance for us?" "I will try my best." "They owe me after a story I did for the Air Force on North Vietnam." "Besides I'm Canadian!" "I was born in this damn country and should get some consideration for that!" Miller said.

The next morning the chopper was waiting and off they all went. As they approached the landing field on Mackenzie Island they could see the CNN tents set up. "The crew is already here." Dan Miller said. "I'm getting that bad old feeling again." Bill Wilson said. "This feels an awful lot like Area 51 and all the Air Force cover ups." "This is my story damn it!" "I will not be pushed around by some Air Force clown or bullshit by bloated bureaucrats." "These damned flunkies can go screw themselves!" Jake said. They took the chopper over to Herschel Island and saw the Air Force tents set up as a headquarters. After they landed they approached the headquarters tent with Major Jesse Armstrong in command. "Sir the CNN people are here," "Thank you captain." The major said. "Alright Mr. Miller and the rest of you." "This is an Air Force operation and I am in charge." "I will allow you to see the crash site, but all stories and photo's go through me." "Is that clear." They all agreed and proceeded to the crash site.

Walking down to the crash was not easy as Air Force check points were in place and the group was stopped every 10 yards. The security guards were ordered to ask for IDs at each stop. Finally, Dan just held his letter from the major up and the group was allowed to proceed. He had a hand written pass from the major and no one dared to question that. The wind was howling and it was damned cold. "What the hell is the temp?" Jake asked a security guard. "It's 40 below and a cold front is moving in." The men were not prepared for the extreme arctic temps. Jake and Suzie had fur coats and hats, but their hands and feet were cold. Dan Miller and

Bill Wilson had CNN insulated boots and gloves, but no fur coats. The Air Force people had Air Force issue arctic coats which are best for these temps. Frozen fog, or rime ice covered everything. The camera lens were frozen and useless. The tape recorders were frozen too. Jake had an old Polaroid camera that was not frozen. "This cheap camera is out performing the newest high tech ones." He bragged. He had one role of film left. "Dan we have got to roll the film and tape." A frustrated Jake yelled out. "Then thaw the damn things out!" Suzie said. "Use these heaters." Dan said. The large alien spacecraft was now visible to them. "It sure looks familiar!" Suzie said. "Yea, just the same as the others." Jake told the group. The smell of burnt metal filled the air and a gray, oily mist burnt their noses. "These symbols are the same as Roswell." Bill said. " We think they are in four groups." "Propulsion, weapons, atmospheric controls, and anti gravity." "But, we never were able to interpret them accurately." "The alien writing is the key to understanding this whole UFO enigma." Bill said. "We may never understand their writing." "Or is it really some man made fake writing made to look like alien writing?" Jake asked. "That way we report it as an alien spacecraft, not a U.S. Experimental aircraft that crashed." "The problem with your theory is that we have never been able to fly the damned UFOs that we reverse engineered." Bill said. "Maybe we can now Bill." Suzie said.

"Those portable heaters should help." Dan said. "Yea, that was damned kind of the Air Force to put them there." Jake said. "Now that we're inside the damned thing what the hell do we do." Dan said. "Film and record." Jake said. "We need proof." "I don't understand why the Air Force let us in." Dan said. "Simple." "The big cover up theory from the fifties." "They are trying to deny it." Bill said. "Well, deny it or not the cameras are now rolling." Jake said as he filmed the entire alien space craft inside and out. The CNN cameras and recorders were now working. "This is Dan Miller reporting for CNN from inside of an alien spacecraft in the Arctic." "As you can see the spacecraft is quite alien and strange looking." "I have with me Bill Wilson from the Roswell and Area 51 days." "Bill what is it?" "Dan, it appears to be similar to the alien spacecraft at Roswell." "Do you mean they came back?" "Perhaps." He continued the dialog and the filming continued. "This will be on tonight." Dan said.

"The anti grav engines over there are like the Roswell UFO too." Bill said. "They can make right turns on a dime." "That is the laser cannon." "The Air Force fired one at Area 51." "It scared the hell out of us." "That is the nuclear reactor." Bill said pointing to a small alien looking machine. "Just like Roswell." "So where will this alien spacecraft go to Area 51?" Suzie said. "They will never tell us that." Bill said. "But, I can say for sure this spacecraft is not a man made craft." "The alien writing proves it is not man made." "Let's get out of here." "That gas is making me sick." Jake said."That smell is like nothing I've ever smelled."

As they left the crash site a fog bank moved in and concealed the entire area. Dan was still filming and recording everything. They returned in the morning and continued filming and recording. Dan had called the story in already and it appeared on the CNN morning report. "This is Dan Miller reporting from Herschel Island again." "We are at the crash site on Herschel Island and that is the alien spacecraft." "As you can see it is a strange looking craft with alien symbols." "USAF officials have refused comment on the downing of the alien spacecraft." "It crashed to earth and that is all we know." "CNN signing off for now." "Now what?" Suzie asked. "We camp out and watch." Jake said. As they returned to their tents at Mackenzie Bay a huge Air Force chopper hovered overhead. "Good job on that report Dan." Jake said. "Yea, I enjoyed it." Bill said. "How about some lunch?" Dan said. They sat down to steak and eggs at the CNN tent. "Now this is living." Suzie said. "Considering where we are this is pretty damned good." Jake said. "All the comforts of home." Suzie said.

It had begun snowing and the area was covered by evening. "They say a blizzard is expected by tomorrow afternoon." Dan said. "Well, we're snowed in." He said. "I'm not going anywhere." Jake said. Jake got them playing a friendly game of black jack. "Damn, Miller how do you get five card naturals every time you try!" Jake asked. "Must be that I live right Green!" "Okay, let's not get personnel!" By midnight they were all broke except Dan and all pretty wasted.

The next morning the fog had lifted and they could see the island. "Take a look over there!" Dan said. "Is that huge chopper doing what I think?" He asked. As they watched with stunned expressions on their faces the huge Air Force chopper lifted the entire spacecraft off the island and headed out. "Let's go baby!" Jake said. They all piled into the CNN Land Rover and took off in the direction of the chopper. "You know that Eskimo village we saw on the way in?" Jake asked. "That's the perfect place to hide the damned thing." "Yea, they had early warning radar there during the entire cold war period." Bill said. The road was icy and had six inches of fresh powder snow on it. "How fast can this thing go Dan?" Jake asked. "About as fast as you're going!" Dan yelled above the roar of the motor. As the CNN cameras rolled taking shots of everything the Land Rover slid off the road. "Just throw her in four wheel drive and off we go." Jake said. "What a way to start the day." "No coffee!" Suzie said. "No problem, I brought the Yukon Jack." Jake said. "Bill want a hit?" "No thanks I never drink on the job." "This doesn't count." Jake said. They all started laughing and the party had begun.

Six hours later and exhausted they pulled back into the CNN tent city. "They hid the damn thing pretty well." Bill said. "Where's the Jim Beam Jake?" Suzie asked.

The next morning it snowed again and the crew was grounded. "Can we get to the island Dan?" Jake asked. "Yea, let's go." "Bring the Geiger counter Bill." Once at the island Bill picked up a lot of background radiation. "That's why they lifted it out of here." "It's radioactive." Bill said. "So, are we infected Bill?" "No." "It's background radiation and not going to harm us." "The reactor must not have been damaged in the crash." "There would be radioactive fall out if it was." "I feel that old deja vu again." Bill said. "You mean it's Roswell all over again?" Dan asked. "Yea, and now we may never find out the truth about these UFOs." Bill said. "Let's get the hell out of here." Jake yelled as they took off.

CHAPTER 6:

THE CRASH WITH NO NAME

"In the desert you can't remember your name cause there ain't no one there to cause you no pain." As Jake's eight track played the "America" song he and Suzie drove through the desert near Needles in his van. Jake and Suzie were on a sort of vacation from news reporting. After being harassed by Air Force Security cops and just about everyone else in Canada they needed a break. After all, the Air Force has been covering up UFO sightings for about fifty years and nobody was too worried about it. Plus, the military and government scientists had been blowing the world all to hell with nuclear weapons for the same length of time. So, it wouldn't hurt anyone if they took a little vacation. "Damn I'm glad to be home." He told Suzie. "It is so warm and wonderful here." She said smiling. "Yea, and I like the bikini you're wearing." "Jake if your thinking what I think your thinking forget it!" She said laughing. "What's that baby?" "I'm talking about the huge bulge in your pants." "Oh, that?" "Maybe we better check into that motel Jakester." "Okay baby, whatever you say." They checked into the "Lamplight Motel" in the desert.

"Hey, it's got a nice big pool and a bar!" Suzie yelled. "That's the ticket baby." "First come here baby." Jake said to Suzie while standing naked in the motel room. "I don't know if I dare!" She said smiling. Later they were in the bar sipping tequila sunrises. "Do you really think we'll find anything?" She asked. "No, probably not." "But, it sure will be fun trying baby!"

The next day they were on old route 66 and the eight track was blaring an Eagles song. "Yea I'm already gone and I'm feeling strong. I will sing this song, cause I'm already gone." "Let's just say no to drugs." Suzie said as Jake lit up a jay. "Okay baby whatever you say." "Why are we headed towards Victorville?" "To check it out." Jake said. "Here we go again." They camped outside the fence and watched the hanger where the UFO had once been. After three days they gave up and packed it in and headed home to Jake's pad in Fairfield. "I guess I need a new career." Jake told Suzie. "Maybe you could work at Disney World." "Yea, the space and alien ride." Jake said laughing. Just then the phone rang. It was Dan Miller and a new UFO sighting was reported to CNN. "It's in Anchorage, Alaska." Dan told Jake. "I'm wiring you money for air fare and hotel, etc. in Anchorage." "Let me know as soon as you get set up and we'll join you." "We're on it." Jake said.

They took Western Airlines to Anchorage International Airport and rented an "FBI" Ford. Elmendorf Air Force Base is the home of the Alaskian Air Command. After snooping around for a few days they rented a house on First street in Anchorage. The house was a ranch style with a nice kitchen, living room and basement with a gas heater. "We'll carpet the basement and make it a music room." Suzie said. It was November and getting very cold in Alaska. "For Thanksgiving I know a great way to cook a turkey." Jake said. "You put it in a large paper bag and cook it in low heat." "It's very moist." "Right!" Suzie said. "It will catch on fire!" "You have to use an oven bag!" "Reynolds Oven Bags numb nuts." "Not paper bags, you character." "Oh, sorry baby." The house was near to the base and several restaurants including a Kentucky Fried Chicken. During the Winter in Alaska it is dark about 20 out of the 24 hours in a day. That made their job of UFO investigating easy. Chilcoot Charles bar was their favorite hangout. Peanut shells on the floor from years of use. They toured the glaziers, salmon runs, blue icebergs and Eskimo bars.

Life in Alaska was okay for awhile for Jake and Suzie, but it can get boring living there and you get cabin fever. "It's too damned cold up here for me Jake." "Yea and we're headed back to the Mojave asap." Jake said. "Let's go to the airport and watch the jets leave for the lower 48." Suzie said. "I'm too depressed for words." "Okay baby." "Roll a dubee baby and we'll check it out." They rode around listening to Jethro Tull and Dave Mason. "These Brit bands are the best rockers," Suzie said. "No way!" "I still like Chuck Berry." Jake said. "That figures Jake cause you're still living in the fifties!"

"Those were the days too baby." "I think we've got cabin fever Jake." "It's high time we got the hell out of here." "So where the hell is this UFO?" She asked.

One morning Jake woke up from a dream and told Suzie about it. "Suzie wake up." "What is it Jake?" "I had this weird dream." "I was in my office at work somewhere, I don't know where. I noticed that I had two baggies full of pot in the cabinet." "I grabbed them before anyone could notice and put them under my shirt". "The woman I was talking with may have seen this, so I tried to find somewhere to go and hide the stuff." "I kept thinking the baggies would fall out of my shirt. I was really paranoid and couldn't find any place private because there were these kids and parents everywhere." "I got outside and hopped over a small fence. I hid behind a pine tree near a gym attached to a school." "Then I remembered I had two more baggies of pot in my briefcase!" "It was in the office." "What do you thing?" "I think you're paranoid of the Air Force." She said with an evil grin.

One night after driving around Anchorage while parked near the Air Force base flight line a huge roar and bright lights came from the sky high above them. Six F-15's scrambled and kicked in their after burners causing the mountains to humble. A loud bang went echoing through the valley as they broke the sound barrier. Another bright light filled the night sky above them and what looked like rockets were being fired from the fighter jets. "Look!" "There are at least two huge aircraft coming down right over our heads!" Jake yelled to Suzie. Then a loud bang as the mass of twisted metal slammed into the runway. There was fire and smoke everywhere. "No one could have survived that." Suzie said. "Oh yea, well what is that?" Several little creatures crawled out of the UFO and on to the ground. Jake was busy filming and taping the whole thing while Suzie looked through the binoculars. Fire trucks came screaming up and put the fires out. An ambulance came and picked up the alien's bodies and drove off. "Did you get all that Jake?" "Yep." More F-15's came streaking past and flew straight up into the night sky as though to do a victory roll. "Look baby you take off and call it in to CNN and Dan while I stay here and film it all." "Check the local hospital and over at the base for the aliens." She drove off and Jake hid himself in the bushes. More Air Force security appeared and put up police tape. Jake was still filming from behind some trees and out of sight of the security. Suzie returned and they took off. They headed home in a hurry. "Jake they brought the alien bodies some where else." "There was no sign of them at the hospital." "We'll have to let Dan at CNN know right away baby." Jake called Dan from home. "I don't know Dan." "It could be a an alien spacecraft like at Herschel Island." "The electromagnetic field the UFOs give off may have downed the jets too." "The UFOs use it as a propulsion system and it interferes with our aircraft." "It's the anti gravity engines that Bill told us about at Herschel Island." "Right Jake I remember." Dan said. "It's all on film and we're sending it to you." "We're leaving before we get busted again." "Okay Jake and keep in touch."

They took the next Western Airlines flight to San Fran. Once in the air they breathed a sigh of relief. "Well, we made it without getting caught this time Jake." "That's right baby." On TV in Jake's pad they watched as Dan Miller described the footage. "This is CNN with Dan Miller reporting." A voice announced. "Hello out there CNN viewers." "Please watch this film carefully." "The footage you're about to see is genuine." "It appears to be a damaged UFO and wrecked Air Force jet." "Several USAF jets shot down the UFO and apparently a jet was downed by the alien craft." "Mr. and Mrs. Jake Green filmed this in Anchorage, Alaska at an Air Force base." Dan said. "What the hell is he doing!" Jake said. "Come on baby let's boogie on out of here." "I'm not going back to the torture chamber." She yelled to Jake. "Hopefully we can stay at least one step ahead of them." Jake said. "You're damned right!" She yelled as they headed out the door.

CHAPTER 7:

"BRING LAWYERS, GUNS AND MONEY"

"Look baby I'm calling my damned lawyer." "I'm tired of running and hiding from these bastards." "Go ahead Jake." Suzie said. "Hello Ben." "This is Jake Green." "Oh you did." "Hello Ben, Ben." "He hung up on me baby." "One of my lawyers for 20 years Ben Beagle hung up on me." "That's gratitude for you." "Look we're like wanted men now Jake." "What do you expect?" They were staying in a hotel near Needles and out of the spying eyes of the FBI and Air Force. "They can't just keep harassing us." Jake said. "Yes they can and yes they will!" "So figure out how we escape this time genius!" "Well I'm changing my name and going back to law school." Jake said. "Okay, I'm with you." Suzie agreed. They were ready to try anything to escape the damned Air Force and FBI.

South Royalton, Vermont has a small law school called, of all things,Vermont Law School. Jake was now "Paul Hudson" and Suzie was his wife Suzie Hudson." "I always wanted to be a lawyer." Jake told his "wife". "Yea right." "A crooked one at that." She said. "Anyway, they'll never find us here." "Plus, I will sue the bastards for what they did to you baby." Suzie was working at the Holiday Inn and Jake had a job writing for a local paper. "What kind of cases are you interested in Jake." " Corporate greed!" " Yea, and White collar crimes." Jake said laughing. Life had slowed down to a trickle for Jake and Suzie. "Jake I am really bored." "Can we go do something!" "Like what baby?" "Damn it Jake I don't care just get me out of here!" "Okay you name it baby." Finally, Jake thought of an idea. "We'll go hunting in the Northeast Kingdom!" Suzie threw a frying pan at him and it hit up side the head. "Now can we go some where?" As the months went by in sleepy Vermont and Jake and Suzie blended in with the local Vermonters it finally happened. Jake filed a law suit against the United States Air Force! That is, he did it in his classroom at school. Jake argued a case against the government in reference to an allegation of kidnapping and torture. Although it was a college exercise it got media attention. Dan Miller saw it on the wire and contacted Jake right away. "That was pretty good Mr. Hudson." "Alright Miller you found me." "That's correct my fine feathered friend who abandoned me on the UFO case!" "I realize you were worried you'd get busted again." "So how's Vermont and when are we invited?" "You and Bill Wilson are welcome anytime." "Good, and we'll be there this coming weekend." "Bring some of that wine you got from Paris when you covered the Eiffel Tower hostage case." "You remember that one?" "Yea, of course and I'll see you guys soon."

"Look baby we need a change of scenery." "I'm even looking forward to seeing Dan and Bill." Jake said to his bored "wife". I graduate next month and want to split." "Now that you're a lawyer you can go anywhere." She said. "Yea right, with no money and the FBI and Air Force looking for us!" "Oh come on Jake." "Be courageous and take a chance." "And I'll blame you if I get busted!" She laughed at the legal beagle and said, "sue me F. Lee Bailey."

When Dan and Bill came to Jake's graduation from law school they did some scheming. "I'm filing a suit in federal court to force the Air Force to tell the truth about the UFO crashes." Jake said. "Okay, man and I'll cover the story." "But, they'll tie it up in court." Dan said. Finally, the case was scheduled for a hearing in federal court in Burlington. Dan interviewed Jake for CNN. "Mr Green, as we stand on the court house steps please tell our viewers about the law suit." "It's about kidnapping, torture and cover ups by the Air Force." "Can you be more specific." Dan asked Jake. "Suzie was kidnapped and tortured because she saw a UFO." "I have film and audio recordings of Air Force jets shooting down UFOs." "Will this be introduced as evidence in court?" "Yes, it will."

The day Jake and Suzie testified Major Armstrong from Air Force Security was present. While they were telling their story about the kidnapping and torture, he was busy writing something down in his notebook. Jake being a lawyer got to cross examine him under oath. "Major Armstrong tell the court everything you know about the UFO crashes." "Everything I know?" "Yes sir." "There wasn't any." "Sir are you telling this court that you know nothing about any UFO crashes?" "That is correct." "Isn't it a fact that the Air Force has a secret facility in Nevada called Area 51?" "I can't say due to national security." "You mean you won't say correct sir?" "National security, Mr. Green is something that you know nothing about." "Your honor please instruct the witness to answer yes or no to questions." The judge refused to do it and the case dragged on.

The hearings went on for several more days with Jake introducing the film and audio recordings of the UFOs. The Air Force denied everything. They explained the films as fakes and the audio as jet noise. Jake couldn't prove anything and the Air Force hid behind national security. The case was dismissed and the newspapers ran a story about how Jake had wasted the courts time and money. Now Jake was being followed again and was paranoid. "I did manage to get the story out to the public." Jake told Suzie. "I'm afraid we have to hide out again though baby."

"First things first baby I've got a plan." "We're going to visit an old friend of mine In Beatty, California.." "It will kill two Air Force birds with one Jake Green stone." "You see baby, he lives near Nellis AFB. They headed West on I-80 and took I-40 to Needles, California. "We're going to Needles first and I have an idea that something is going down there."

As they drove through Needles Jake got that old deja vu feeling. "Keep your eyes peeled honey." "What the hell am I looking for Jake?" "I'm not sure." They located a huge warehouse near some railroad tracks. "This freaking warehouse is at least 500 yards long and about three stories tall." Jake said. "From the looks of how full the parking lot is there must be 5000 workers on all three shift, seven days a week." "Something damn big is happening here." They parked the "FBI car" within eyesight of the huge building and at about 3am a train pulled in. "They're unloading trailers by the dozen." "The workers look like freaking zombies or robots." Suzie said quietly."If that's what I think it is honey...." Jake said. "I'm sneaking over there for a look see." Jake managed to find some work cloths and an ID and got changed. He pretended to be a worker and walked up to a guy and said, "this go where the rest of the alien wreck is?" "Yea and keep quiet buddy." He followed the others into the basement and couldn't believe his eyes. "There!" "There it is!" "Now I can see why they're so secretive!" A huge pile of twisted alien metal was stacked up to the ceiling. "They've got it all." There were alien looking generators or engines, solar panel looking things, strange looking mirrors, some kind of propulsion or rocket engines, clear glass domes, alien looking controls and much more. "Now I know why they all look like zombies." "The military has brain washed them or drugged them so they won't talk to anyone about any of this." He was taking a load of photos while he spoke into the mini recorder on his shoulder. Jake sneaked out the same way he came in and rejoined Suzie in the car. "Jake you idiot they're getting suspicious of the car let's go!" "Where the hell were you on the North Pole?" "Yea, and color us gone!"

"Baby that warehouse was loaded with pieces of alien spacecraft and all kinds of alien looking things." "I got it all on film." "Now I know why Needles is so damned strange!" Jake said. As they drove along the highway the workers back in the warehouse were finishing piecing back together an alien spacecraft. "Well Jimbo we're about finished." "Maybe." An engineer said to his buddy. "Air Force aeronautical engineers will be here by midnight." "They're doing the reverse engineering of the UFO from the blue prints we found inside of the damned thing." "The problem will be figuring out the language it's written in." "Why is that Jimbo asked. "They did it with the same language at Roswell." "Maybe." The engineer said. "The Air Force still doesn't have one of these UFOs that can fly right yet." "Don't worry they'll figure it out sooner or later."

Jake had a friend that ran the Whittier Hotel in Needles and Suzie and he could hide out for awhile. The Red Dog Cafe is one of Jake's old hang outs from his hippie days. After they checked into the Whittier they went over to the cafe for some drinks. "It's been awhile since I've been in here

Jake." "I danced here a couple years ago." "Is there any place you haven't danced?" "Yea, on your head!" "You see that juke box baby." "It's got all my old hippie tunes on it." Jake played a bunch of tunes and they danced. The next morning Jake was all hung over. "Too damn much tequila baby." "You always do that Jake!" "Here." "I made you a Bloody Mary with my secret hangover remedy." "What might that be?" "No way Jose!" "Just drink it down little baby."

Bruce "the Juicer" Polanski was one of Jake's best friends from the old days in the desert. Jake and Suzie caught up with him at lunch at the hotel. He had stayed around in Needles and bought the Whittier. "Bruce, how they been hanging?" Jake asked. "Kind of low down like you my old buddy." "They still call you "Jake the flake?" "Suzie girl did you know your "husband" is called "Jake the Flake?" "Yea." "He earned that name didn't he?" "Especially now girl." "Chasing after UFOs!" "Jake I know damned well that UFOs exist." "Why the hell do you need to prove it?" Juicer said. Jake was cracking up about all the attention he was getting. "Look old buddy." "How'd you like to take a little drive with us?" "Okay flaky." "Where?" "Beatty." "Okay." "I figure we'll take I-40 to Barstow, to Ca., 58 West to Ca. 395 North, to Ridgecrest, to Ca. 178 North to Argus, to Ca. 190 South to Death Valley Jct." "From there Ca. 373 North to Beatty." "Let me guess." "It's right near Nellis AFB." "That's right juicer." "Okay." "I'll load up the Land Rover with supplies right now." Juicer said.

They made it to Ridgecrest the first day and stayed at the "Old Stud Inn". The local paper, "Daily Independent" had a story about UFOs being sighted in the Death Valley area. The story read: "two miners reported seeing several UFOs last night." "Clem Higgins and Jeb Rawley reported it to the Daily Independent." "The miners reported: "We seen em up thar in da sky." Clem said as he was interviewed by Pete Funk from the newspaper. "Sir, what did it look like?" "Twas a silver thang and looked like my first silver strike in '48." Jeb said. "So, what did you both do?" "We was coming inta town fur a grub steak and we was mighty thirsty." "That's when it just bout took Clem's head off!" The rest of the story focused on other past UFO sightings in the area.

"I think we came to the right place." Jake told Suzie and Juicer. They arrived in Argus, California and spent the night at the "Argonian Cafe and Inn." The tequila was good and they slept well. The Argus Courier had a story about three college students you got lost near China Like Naval Weapons Center. The story read: "two boys and one girl became disoriented after taking peyote and were lost." "They wandered on to Naval restricted land and were shot." "The Navy had no comment concerning the incident." "The bodies were picked up by the Dry Desert Funeral Home for burial on boot hill." "Damn is this a joke or what?" Jake said. "Who the hell knows flake." Juicer said. "It could be you next." The story continued to say that Lakehead University President Sir William

Ivory stated the students were good kids and he was shocked by the tragedy. "I say old boy, in my home country of England we don't just bloody kill a bloke for trespassing." "I say it tis rather cowardly and I'd like to tell the bloody Navy about how I bloody feel." The story continued: "three days later Sir Ivory was deported to England." "The British Home Office had no comment." "Damn, those Navy assholes really have some clout." Suzie said.

They arrived in Beatty late the next night and checked into the Stagecoach Motel and Casino. "Well, we're within a stones' throw of Nellis AFB Jake." Juicer said. Neil Young was singing in the background on the juke box and his sad depressing song went on and on. " I went into town to see yesterday but you were not home so I talked some old friends for awhile before I wandered off alone." "It's so hard for me now but I'll make it some how though I know I'll never be the same won't you ever change your ways it's so hard to make the pace when your on the losing end and I feel that way again..." "Are you sure he's Canadian?" Suzie asked. They were sitting in the Lizard Rock Grill and Steak House at the bar. "Neil Young is American." Juicer said. "He's Canadian-American." Jake settled it. "So, tomorrow is business as usual for a traveling salesman and his trainees." Jake said. "We sell rug shampoo machines." "That's our cover." "Here's the free packets and specks." "We go to Nellis and ask them for a pass and then snoop around." "And what happens when we get busted flake?" "We act all innocent and holy." Jake pulled out his Bible and Born Again Christian packets from a suitcase." "You see we are really recruiting for Born Again Christians." "This is the Bible belt and we should be believed." "Suzie has the outfits and we will all look the part." "I've got fake IDs for us and they don't know you juicer." Jake explained. "Yucca Mountain is only 18 miles from here and I know there's a lot of activity there."

They arrived at the gate at Nellis at 9am and were told that no visitors were allowed on base without a pass from the base commander. Major Jesse Armstrong was OD and Jake almost shit when he saw him. "Ah Major ah how are you sir?" "I'm okay Green." "What brings you to Nellis?" "Don't answer that." "They're okay sergeant." "Yes sir." The gate was opened and the three "salesmen" entered the base. Once in the mess hall Major Armstrong told Jake he needed to clear out. "Look Green this is a top secret facility." "Course you're used to hearing that." "Look Major we really appreciate that you let us in here and just want to ask a few questions." Jake said. "Have there been any sightings near the Yucca Mountain storage facility?" "Of course not Green." The major said it in a way that made Jake think he was sending a message. "Thank you sir." "We had better take your advise and leave at once." Once in the car and on their way Jake told Suzie and Juicer they were really on to something. "As a lawyer I can tell you all that we are within our rights as U.S. Citizens to visit this nuclear storage facility." "Is that until we get arrested and are never seen or heard from again?" Juicer asked. The Yucca Mountain storage facility is under ground and basically unapproachable. "We won't get within 10 miles of the place." Suzie said. "That's why we're camping right here." "We'll just be patient and watch and see what happens." Jake said. They had found an oasis and a beautiful spot to camp. "All the comforts of home." After setting up the tents and their filming gear they got a huge fire going."Expect the unexpected." Juicer said. "And we are ready." Jake said. "Steaks or hot dogs?" Jake asked his friends. After three days they were getting restless and wanted some action. "Look, can we go into town?" Suzie asked. "Yea, and we all need a shower and hot baths." Jake said.

Chapter 8:

Seeing the Light and the Rise of "Decker!"

Back at the Stagecoach Motel they all took nice long hot baths. "The water smells a little bit like sulfur, but what the hell." Juicer said. "Yea, but the tequila sunrises are fine!" Suzie said. "Let's go out on the town." Juicer said. "I want to fight, fuck and get drunk!" They went to the Alamogordo Nuke, a local hang out and dance place. Suzie got loaded and started dancing on the bar. "Go girl go!" The locals yelled. She took everything off except her sexy bra and panties. "Okay baby we better go now." Jake said.

Next stop was the Dixie tavern on Furnace street. The locals were mostly miners and old timers. "Hey you mister." "You talking to me?" Jake asked. "Well, I ain't talkin to the wall." "Least not yet." All the miners let out with a laugh. "I don't spose you'd stake me to a grub stake?" "Sure old timer." "How much you need?" "Oh say $25." Jake gave him the money and asked him some questions. "Any UFO flying saucers around here?" "Nope." "Are you sure?" "Yep." They decided to head back to the motel when the old timer said, "hey mister you didn't ask me bout them lights out in the desert." "Okay tell us." "Well they been out thar fur a couple yars naw ." "Thar real purdy and blue and red and all colors." "We like em just fine." "Where in the desert?" Jake asked. "Nar that there Yucca place." "You mean the storage facility?" "Yep." "Thanks old timer." Jake gave him another $20 and they left.

Back at the camp site they did some scheming. "We can get nearer to the facility by traveling at night on horse back." Juicer said. They rented horses and rode closer to the facility at night. It was a night with no moon and very dark. As they approached the facility they saw the lights. "There!" Suzie said. "They are all the colors the old timer said they were." As they filmed the dancing lights in the sky it became apparent that they were UFOs, not Air Force planes. "That's not Saint Elmo's Fire or any natural light show." Juicer said. "We better stick around for awhile." Jake said. Each night the lights got brighter and seemed to be looking at something. "I get the feeling they are watching us." Suzie said. "They probably are." Juicer said. "They are beautiful." He said.

"Yea beautiful." Jake said. "But, their here for some reason." "I think that the nuclear waste is so "hot" and radioactive that it's contaminating our planet." "The aliens or whatever is up in the sky is monitoring it." "This freaking waste dump is a hot bed for all kinds of pollution." "Yea and it lasts for freaking ever." Juicer said.

They filmed the lights for two more nights and returned to Beatty. Jake Called Dan Miller and he was sending a CNN team to film it and report on it. Bill and Dan were on their way.

They returned to the oasis the next night."Major Armstrong must have been telling me something." Jake said. "I think it's the damned nuclear storage facility." Juicer said. "That's what it's been all along." "The damned aliens are afraid that Mankind will pollute the whole damned Universe!" "They may be right!" Suzie said. "We've got to get in there." Juicer said. "You know Juicer you seem to be awfully excited for someone who made fun of all this a couple days ago." Jake said. "I was waiting for you to say that flake." "Anyway, how can we get in there?" "How does anyone get in there?" "They have official passes." Suzie said. "You mean like a Senator would have?" Juicer said. "Exactly." Jake said.

Jake made up a fake pass and dressed in his "FBI" suit and approached the storage facility. At the main gate a guard stopped him. "Sir this is off limits to..." Jake showed the guard the fake pass. "Senator Hudson you may inter." The guard opened the gate. "Okay sarge he can inter the facility." The guard yelled to the sentry. Once inside Jake found a diagram of the entire facility. He toured the place and after three hours was about to leave when he saw an elevator. "I'll take it all the way to the bottom." He found some safety glasses and a radiation badge to wear and proceeded to check it out. "Let's see this room that says top secret is good." As he opened the door alarms started going off. He ran out and headed for the elevator. It was locked down. He ran into a room marked "Do Not Inter." Once inside he could smell that same smell from Herschel Island. It was a huge room and filled with debris from alien spacecraft. There were four huge freezers with alien bodies in them. He grabbed for his camera and snapped off a dozen pictures. He was recording all the while and speaking into the tiny microphone on his shirt. "I'll take some tissue samples and a few pieces of the space craft and be on my way."He saw another sign that read: "radioactive waste." Since he had a radioactive badge he entered the area. He found a Geiger counter and began testing the area for radioactive contamination. "It's hot alright." He said as the Geiger counter began registering in the positive hot zone on the meter. "But, where is the hot contamination coming from. The large area he was in had nothing in it except piping and air vents. "These pipes must come from underground." He left the area and located an office nearby. On the wall was a chart of all nuclear waste transports to date. "It has some with red stars near them." "I wonder what that means?" "It appears to be some kind of trouble during transport of the nuclear waste material." "I count 45 red stars." "That means that 45 transports of nuclear waste were either spilled or leaked or something." "That's terrific!" "Now they're polluting our entire country side with nuclear waste which lasts for thousands of years!" "Radioactive waste can last for hundreds of thousands of years." "It comes from spent fuel rods and old nuclear weapons." "They had planned to store it under ground, above ground, under the sea, in space, in warehouses and any where else they could hide it." "In Russia there have been "accidents" where huge spills of this waste has gone into lakes and rivers." "The stuff can be stolen and "Dirty Bombs" made.   He took pictures of everything and decided to get moving.

Out the door he flew and up the emergency stairway he went. "I'm on my way to Hollywood as a big shot news correspondent or better still a movie star!" When he returned to the motel Jake burst into the room where Suzie was and started telling her what happened. "I, I got it all on film Suzie." "I saw it all in a secret basement." "There was alien bodies and UFO debris." "The worst thing was all the nuclear waste pollution." Juicer came bursting and asked what happened. "Juicer I got it all man!" They all hopped into the Land Rover and headed for LA to develop the film. "Let's get out right away." Jake said. "They ain't getting my film!"

Dan and his CNN Team arrived the next day and they all set up in the desert ."This is Dan Miller for CNN reporting from the desert near Yucca Mountain Nuclear Storage Facility." "The lights you see are believed to be UFOs." "Bill Wilson is on hand to comment." "Bill what are those lights?" Well, Dan they appear to be the same lights that have been appearing around this area for quite some time." "There movement indicates they are some kind of aircraft." "They appear to be watching the nuclear storage facility."

Inside the facility Air Force brass were meeting. "Major Armstrong has our security been breached?" "I'm afraid so General Westmorland." "You will move everything to a new location by dawn." "Yes sir General." "About these UFO lights in the sky major." "Yes sir." "The Special Ops unit is preparing to take them out now." "See that it's done Major." "Yes sir."

Now that they were on the run again Suzie and Jake ran out of money fast. Jake was back to news reporting and Suzie dancing. They were camped out in Williams, Arizona below the Grand Canyon. Flagstaff, Winslow, and the towns along the old route 66 were their news beat. Suzie was dancing at a club in Winslow and at a dance studio in Flagstaff. She was teaching young girls the dance moves they'd need to earn a living. Jake covered anything that looked like news. He had been down to Phoenix at Luke Air Force base snooping around one day when a hanger blew up. Jake was on the story in seconds. He had camera's, tape recorders and all his interviewing skills ready to go. "Excuse me Major Armstrong, what caused the fire?" "You look familiar." "Well, I'm a CNN reporter now sir." "Oh alright then." "Fuel ignited in the hanger and blew the doors off." "Were any planes damaged in the explosion?" "Yes, there were two jet tankers in there and they caught fire too." "Is the fire out?" "Yes, and everything is under control." "Now if you'll excuse me sir." The major left and Jake went snooping around the hanger. The hanger doors were still smoking and soot covered everything. "What the hell, I'll just wait in the car for the smoke to clear and then go in the hanger." Jake had the "FBI" Ford and his FBI dressed in blue suit on. It was getting dark and the airmen had left the area and Jake moved in. He recorded as he sneaked around the hanger. "This is Jake Green reporting for CNN from Luke Air Force Base in Glendale, Arizona." "There was a huge fire here after an explosion in a hanger." "It blew up two jet tankers and the hanger doors were blown off." "As you can see the fire is out." "I am approaching the empty hanger now." "The debris from the explosion is on the hanger floor and wait...!" "There appears to be shiny metal and parts of a glass dome on the floor." "The smell of the burning metal is familiar to me from covering a story in Canada." "It was a UFO crash site near MacKenzie Bay in the Yukon Territory." "On Herschel Island we filmed the crash and recorded it for CNN." Since the hanger doors were blown off they couldn't close them and Jake had finally gotten his news story. As he panned his camera around the scene in the hanger and the film rolled, he felt like a real reporter for the first time. "As you can see the debris on the hanger floor is possibly from a UFO or alien spacecraft." "I wish I could can this smell for you viewers to smell." "So. I will attempt to do just that." He found a piece of plastic and formed it into a sort of container. He placed it over the smoke causing the smell and fill the container. "I will now seal it with duck tape which I always carry with me on these investigations." Several blue Air Force cars had pulled up in front of the hanger. "Sir, you are on USAF property without the commanders permission." A security policeman said. "I was just leaving and thank you."

There are several Air Force bases in the area. Davis-Monthan, near Tucson, Williams AFB, 30 miles from Phoenix, Kirtland near Albuquerque, Hollomon near Alamogordo and Cannon near the Texas panhandle. Jake had done his research and decided to investigate all of them. But, first he was off to Alamogordo, New Mexico to investigate the site of the first atomic bomb test. "It was July 16, 1945 in the desert sixty miles South West of Roswell." "They detonated the first atomic bomb." Jake said to himself while scheming. "All top secret." Jake figured he was on to something. "Then two years later the Roswell UFO incident." "Coincidence?" "No way in hell!" "Roswell AFB was the home of the Enola Gay, the B-29 bomber that dropped the first A-Bomb on Japan." "Then UFOs are sighted and aliens found there." "Not a coincidence!" "I can actually visit the site of the first damned atomic bomb test blast two days out of the year." "Trinity!" "It's near here." "Tomorrow just happens to be one of those days!" Jake headed East on route 66, (now I-40) to I-25 to route 70 and White Sands Proving Grounds. "There was the UFO sighting at White Sand too." Jake remembered. "I'll camp out and check the whole damned place out." "This time I go alone." "I'll call Suzie from White Sands."

Jake was at his best while scheming, but could he actually follow a plan through to the finish?.

"Somehow this is all tied together." As Jake drove along route 66 he went over every piece of evidence he had regarding the UFOs. He had sent the alien skin tissue, clothing sample and alien metal from the space craft he got to a lab for analysis. They reported that it came from an unknown source. The evidence was piling up fast and Jake knew he was on to a big story. Plus, Jake had found out something really important about UFOs, the Air Force, Suzie, CNN, the law suit and all the traveling around. He knew that covering these sightings and reporting it was exciting and he loved it. "I think I've found myself in all this." He mused. "There's something about it that I love." "I don't want to mind fuck it and the feeling I have now is good enough." "I don't need to think anymore about it either." "I'm a damned news hound." Jake knew that being a newsman is really being a news "correspondent." A "journalist". "Reporters", are old school." He told himself with a laugh. "Hey!" "I'm not laughing at myself for a change!" "Damn, I must be on the right path."

Driving straight across the Southwest in his FBI Ford was not bad for Jake. "I've got the AC on and cruise control set a 80 mph." "I'll be there in no time." It was 3am when he finally arrived at White Sands. He camped out for the first night and called Suzie the next day. "Hey baby." "Guess where I am?" "Jake you took off on your "wife." "No honey I'm on a new case." "Then you're at some Air Force base, right?" "Well, very near to one." "I'm at White Sands." "Don't tell CNN or anyone baby." "I'm snooping around out here where the first atom bomb test was." "Trinity!" "It was called Trinity baby!" "What a name for a deadly nuclear weapon!" Suzie said. "The Trinity of the Catholic Church is The Father, The Son and The Holy Spirit." She told Jake. "Only now it's a damned bomb site!" She said with anger. "Okay baby now calm down." "When are you coming home Jake?" "Listen, baby I know all of the UFO and Air Force cover ups are related to Trinity and Roswell." "I've got to find proof." "Okay, then I'll be out there in two days." "Are you sure about this baby?" "Yea." "I'm positive." "That's what I love about you baby." "A positive lover."

The next morning while it was still dark he tested the sand and other objects with his Geiger counter. "No background radiation." "That doesn't mean it's safe here though!" "Bill said the stuff lasts for thousands of years." "The aliens who landed in Roswell must have known something about all this." "They were here for a reason." "Now the Air Force wants to blow them out of the sky." "The aliens could be a little pissed off about their brothers being killed by Earthmen." "Reverse engineering." "Creating new more advance things from stolen alien technology." "Like the stealth fighter and the computer chip!" "I wonder how we created atomic energy and bombs." "Maybe we stole that too!" Jake was on to something. "That small nuclear reactor on the UFO at Herschel Island." "Bill knew all about that." "I say we reverse engineered it from the 1941 Cape Girardeau UFO that we recovered." "Then we developed the Atomic Bomb!" "The aliens wanted to prevent that from happening." "They knew how crazy humans are and didn't trust them with atom bombs." The problem for Jake was proof. "I can't prove a damned thing!" "Unless I can find one of the alien UFOs intact." "That's what the hell I'm doing here!"

Jake had been at White Sands for two whole days and had seen nothing. "What the hell is that jeep doing driving over here?" "Damn, it's Suzie!" As the jeep CJ5 pulled up to Jake's tent he saw the women he loved. She had a tight fitting top on and her boobs practically fell right out of it. Her shorts were skin tight and her beautiful, full butt stuck out a mile. She smiled that sexy, Suzie smile and Jake called out to her. "Hey baby!" "Get over here and come to daddy!" "Okay you crazed wild man!" Jake hauled off and kissed her for about five hours non stop. "So what the hell is this all about Jake?" "You'll see baby."

"You see Suzie, one day a man copied something from another person." "Then we created spying." "You know like on the Commies." "Then one day a UFO crashed in America and the brilliant scientist geeks found a little, funny looking machine called a nuclear reactor on the space ship from the stars." "They eventually figured out how to copy it and we got atomic bombs!" "Any questions?" "Well, the crazy aliens didn't understand human greed and deceit and kept coming back to Earth." "But, the scientists had already gotten all they could from them and didn't need them anymore." So, the Air Force and who knows who else started blasting them out of the sky!" "Then we came along and now we're wanted dead or alive." "They need to get rid of us!" "Jake you think we copied atomic energy from the aliens?" "Yea baby I do." "What about the Russians and other countries with nukes?" "They had spies!" "Now I need some proof." "We have to capture an alien UFO intact and show the world what really happened." "Then the UFO mystery will finally be solved." "We can show how Mankind tried to do it again." "We tried to kill off another species to make way for our own greedy, selfish species, called MAN!"

"Here at White Sands is where it all started." "July, 1945 the first big atomic blast." "I say the aliens knew all about it and wanted to warn us to stop the program." "But, we had already gotten their secrets from them and ignored them." "Now, whenever they come to Earth we take them out!" "But, they keep coming." "This is where they want to visit." "Right here where we're standing." "So we're camping out right here until hell freezes over if we have to." "They'll be back, don't worry baby." Jake had filled his car with supplies and camping gear. "We've got Denny Moore Beef Stew tonight baby." He had a camp fire going and figured if it attracted attention he'd say they were just camping." "Hell, what more can a guy ask for?" Nine hours later as the sun began to rise Jake's tape deck was still playing music. "It's another tequila sunrise this old world still seems the same another frame..."

Jake was passed out in his sleeping bag and Suzie is hers. Little did they realize that a white Jeep was parked nearby with Air Force security police who had been watching them. Holloman AFB was a few miles away and a busy place. Experimental aircraft were warming up and ready to go. SR-71 "Blackbirds" were fueled and on the flight line. As they slammed into the early morning sky and kicked on the huge continuous bleed afterburning turbojets the ground shook and mother nature shuttered. At 80,000 feet and 2200 mph the monsters kept climbing and had a plan. First tested at Area 51, (Groom Lake), in 1962 and deployed for high altitude recon the SR-71 Blackbird was never shot down by enemy fire. The only thing faster was the experimental X-15 rocket powered spacecraft which clocked a speed of over 4500 miles per hour! But, the SR-71 Blackbird could out run any UFOs! The pilot of one of the huge monster jets radioed in to Base Ops. "Cap K and group climbing out on vector Charlie-Romeo at Two, Five, Zero climbing to One, Two, Zero on Laser Vecter" "Wilco Cap K nothing on your six." "Zulu, Victor, Wilco and out." With no traffic ahead or behind, the Blackbirds kicked it up mach 3. A terrible roar shook the desert far below. Able to out run anything in the sky the Blackbirds ruled Earth and space.

Jake awoke to the thunder high above him and jumped up. "Wow!" "That was something mighty big!" "Think I'll go snoop around." "Suzie." "I'm going over to the base and check that sonic boom out." "Okay Jake." As he drove off towards the base he could feel the ground shake again. After he got a visitors pass at the gate he went for a coffee at the mess hall. Since he was a Vietnam Era Vet and Air Force medic in a prior life he knew his way around Air Force bases. " There's a hell of a lot of activity going on here and I want to know why." He told himself as he drank his coffee. The problem for Jake and all the other UFO investigators is that USAF bases are usually always busy. So, it is impossible to know what is really going on. That's exactly what they want. All he could do is watch and wait. Suddenly a voice came over the loud speakers. "We have a priority one alarm." "All personnel report to duty stations immediately." "I repeat priority one alarm." "All liberty and leaves are canceled as of 7:23 hours." Jake knew that it was a plane crash. "But, where the hell is it!" He asked himself in a panic. "I'm going to get Suzie and check this out." He quickly left the base and drove to where they were camped. "Suzie come on it's a crash."

A large area was on fire off to the East of their camp site. "Come on baby we're on to another one." As they approached the crash site Jake could make out two separate crashed planes. "That looks like an SR-71 and and some experimental aircraft." He told Suzie. "Sorry folks this is strictly off limits to civilians." An Air Force SP told them. "I'm from CNN and covering the story." Jake said as he showed the SP his credentials. "Then stay behind the yellow police tape please." Suzie had set up the camera and began taping. There was debris all over about a 100 yard area with fires and black smoke billowing out into the morning air. Several fire trucks were spraying foam on the fires and an ambulance was loading the airman's bodies onto stretchers. Suddenly a huge disc shaped UFO came screaming past overhead. It made no sound and disappeared into the dark blue sky. "Let's go baby." "We got a live one!" Jake yelled out. As he drove across the desert in pursuit of the UFO Jake remembered the Major at MacKenzie Bay. "You know that Major Armstrong was not a bad sort of person." "I really can't say Jake." Suzie said. "Jake we've got company." Several white jeeps were on their ass and had their flashing lights on. "Pull over Jake!" Suzie said. Four Air Force security policemen jumped out of the jeeps and approached Jake's car. Sergeant Decker was head of security for the base and said, "didn't we see you around here before?" "Well, we camped out here." "Never mind just get out and assume the position." "You two are under arrest for trespassing on government property." "Put the cuffs on them and throw in the jeep." "Hey sarge this one is a smart ass." A security cop told Decker. "Oh really." "Bring him over here." "Look fuck face I don't like you or your spying little bastard friends." Decker punched Jake in the gut. "Hey sarge what are we going to do with this asshole spy?" "Well I just don't know private." "What did you have in mind?" "How about a Laredo Suntan." He said laughing hysterically. "Yea." Decker said. "Tie him behind the Jeep private." "Yes sir I'm looking forward to this." They dragged Jake behind the Jeep and then untied him. "Well shit head do we feel a little less smart ass now?" Decker asked. Jake said, "I want to see your commanding officer." "Oh you do, do you." "Take him for another little ride private." "Yes sir!" After another Laredo Suntan Jake passed out. "Throw some water on him." Decker said. After Jake came around Decker asked him, "now shit for brains are we more comfortable?" Decker asked laughing. "I think he's had it sarge," The private said. "Yea. He's all tuckered out." "I'll bet he has a limp dick don't he girl?" Decker asked Suzie. "Damn what a fucking waste of humanity this fucker is." Decker said." "Now get them the fuck out of here right now I can't stand the sight of either one of them." Decker yelled to his men.

They were driven to bass security and taken to see the OD. "I'm Major Armstrong, have we met before?" "Yes sir at MacKenzie Bay." "Right." "What were you doing on restricted Air Force land?" "Chasing a UFO?" "Alright, Sarge you can go." "Wait a second sir, these two were spying and trespassing." Decker said. "I'm filing charges for spying and whatever else I can charge them with." "Alright Green and Mrs. Green you both need to get the hell away from here right now." "Do you both read me!" "This is an Air Force instillation and not some UFO or flying saucer show on TV." "But, Major that Decker was abusive to Suzie and me!" Jake finally spoke. "Okay Green." "Maybe someday I'll buy you two a beer at the local bar in "gordo". "Okay?" "Goodbye!" "Sergeant take them to the main gate and see that they leave the base immediately." The major told Decker. "Yes sir." Decker grabbed Jake and the other men took Suzie and pushed them towards the door. "Let's go people." Decker yelled. "Now move it Green." At the gate Decker told Jake, "I hope to see you again Green you fucking rat!!" "I'll really kick your dumb ass next time puke face!" "Now get the fuck out of here and don't ever come back!"

Jake and Suzie got the message and later that night met the major at "Nukes-Trinity Bar and Grill" in Alamogordo. While they chowed down on their "Three mile Island Burgers", Jake spoke with Major Armstrong. "Okay here we are major." "I want to help you two and I'll tell what's happening." The Major siad. "Back in 1941 we shot down, a UFO near Cape Girardeau, Missouri." and it had a nuclear reactor which we copied." "We made the atomic bomb and the rest is history." "We copied every thing." "The aerodynamics, computer chips, laser beam, stealth technology, propulsion system, etc." "Now the damn things keep coming back around and we shoot them down." "They have become pests." "Our mission is the defense of this nation, not some UFO hunt." "You got that Green!" "Yes major." "Now what?" Jake foolishly asked the Major. "Now nothing!" "That's it and get the hell out of here for good!" "The Major had spoken the truth." "That can be our lead story Jake." Suzie said after the Major had left.

They went over to Roswell and snooped around. They decided to do a feature story for CNN on the Roswell UFO crash of 1947. Suzie interviewed local folks and Jake filmed the entire thing. After it was completed they called Dan at CNN and wired him the story of the Roswell UFO. "Now I feel more like a normal reporter." Suzie said. "Yea and Dan likes the story that Major Armstrong gave us too." Jake said. On the drive from Roswell to White Sands on route 380 security police pulled them over. "It's Decker." Jake said. Decker and three other SP's walked up to the car and told Jake and Suzie to get out. "Hi puke face." Decker said to Jake. "What part of get the hell out of here don't you two morons understand?" "Don't fucking bother to answer me you hippie, fagot!" "Hey Bob have you ever seen two people more stubborn and simple minded in your life?" Bob, a security police sergeant said, "well sarge I guess not." "What the hell do we do with them?" "Since they're on a honeymoon we'll make sure they have some privacy." Decker went to his Jeep and got a shovel. "Here shit head start digging." Jake refused to dig and Decker got Suzie and brought her over to him. "Bob, take her for a ride in the desert." "Okay sarge." Bob and one of the Security Police took Suzie into the desert while Decker stayed with Jake. "Okay asshole now dig!" Jake refused and Decker punched him in the gut and then pushed him on to the ground. "Hey private get over here." Decker told one of his men. "Yes sir sergeant." "Private." "Fuck head here won't follow orders." "You know what that means." "Yes sir." The private kicked Jake in the side and took the shovel and told him to dig. "Now fucking dig you commie spy!" Jake began digging as they laughed hysterically, "I think he pissed his pants sarge." "Oh no!" "He shit himself too.!" "You are one disgusting piece of shit Green." Decker said. After he had dug down about six feet Decker told him,"okay now make it longer." "It needs to be big enough for you and Mrs. Green." He said laughing. "Well sarge this is one way to get rid of a fucking spy." The private said. "No trial, no prison, no more Green!" Decker said laughing. "Can I get a drink of water?" Jake asked. "Throw some fucking water on him private. Jake jumped up, took the shovel and hit Decker over the head. He jumped in the jeep and sped off. "Suzie will have to send me a signal or something." He said in a panic. He didn't know what the hell to do, so he just kept driving. He was in the White Sands Proving Grounds now and lost.

Meanwhile, Suzie was holding her own too. "Listen fellas I wanted to leave that creep Green anyway and I want to thank you both,." "How'd you like a little strip show?" "Alright miss." Sarge said. Suzie got out of the Jeep and took everything off except her bra and parties. She started dancing real slow and sexy right in front of the cops. Next, off came the bra and off came the panties. While the cops were going completely gaga she jumped into the Jeep bare ass and took off across the desert. "Yippee, coyote!" She screamed. Jake saw the Jeep and headed straight for it. "I'll kick their asses!"

Jake screamed. He was planning to ram them and at the last second he saw his nude "wife". "Baby, why are you buck naked?" "It's a long story and we don't have time now." She jumped into the car and said, "step on Jakester!" As they sped across the desert Suzie put in some music. "People are strange when your a stranger, faces look empty when you're alone. When you're strange faces come out of the rain, when you're strange..." "I always loved the Doors baby." "Good choice."

Chapter 9:

"Poor, Poor Pitiful Me,"
the Fall of Decker!

Jake called Dan Miller and arranged to meet him and Bill at the Grand Canyon. There's a great hotel there and Suzie insisted on a hot bath. They checked into room 420 and smoked the last of Jake's pot while Suzie took her hot bath. "Jake why didn't you bring more dope?" "Do you actually believe Dan or Bill will have any smoke?" "No and I've got a surprise for you." "I've got some legal marijuana." "What!" "That's right baby it's legal." "I got a script back home from my doc." "I told him that I needed it to get a hard on." "You perverted sex fiend!" "And I just smoked some lover." Jake walked into the bathroom bare ass with a huge boner on. "Hi baby, I'm hot for your loving." "Oh my god I guess you are!" Suzie said as he hopped into the tub.

"I'll bet shit for brains Decker is royally pissed off." Jake said to Dan at dinner later that night. "Yea and hot on your asses!" "So now we have a plan." Bill said. "Here it is form the Area 51 man." "We use the CNN jet chopper and search the desert around White Sands, but not on the government reservation." "We listen in on the Air Force frequency for any alerts to do with UFOs." "We locate the UFO before they do and get our alien evidence." "Okay Bill it's approved and we'll get started in the morning." Dan said.

They got going at sunrise and flew over the Grand Canyon. "It's really spectacular!" Suzie said. "This would be a great hiding place for a UFO." As they proceeded to White Sands Bill did some calculating. "I put it at 220 degrees South, Southwest Dan." "Wilco Bill." "We'll do a sweep of the area and return to base camp." Dan said. "It's a mighty big desert from up here." Jake said while scanning the area below with binoculars. "We can call this the CNN, UFO hunt." Suzie said. After three days of patrolling the desert they were ready to give up when Jake saw a silver disk reflect the sunlight. "There." "You guys see it?" "Okay Jake we see it and we're going in for a look." The disc shaped spacecraft was lying in the white, sandy desert. It blended in except for the reflection from the sun. As they landed the chopper Dan told everybody to stay put while Bill checked it out. He carefully approached the silver disk and then motioned for Dan and the camera crew to start rolling the film. "Over here people." Bill said while he tried to open the glass dome. The alien spacecraft was huge. "It must be almost as large as a football field." Jake said. "That's right." "It has to be that large to house the warp drive engines." Bill said. "That is the ion drive engine." Bill was pointing at a huge alien looking machine. "The Ion Drive speeds the craft to almost light speed while in Hyperdrive out in space." "That way the craft can continually accelerate." Bill said. "The warp engines are used to inter a worm hole in space." I know it's all still theory." Bill said. "That is beyond our technology." "But, they are the same warp engines that were on the Roswell spacecraft." "That unit in the back of the craft is the Anti Gravity Engines." "It allows the craft in escape Earth's atmosphere." 'The metal it is made of is light in weight." "But, stronger then anything we have." "They have an atomic or nuclear powered drive too." "That's what we copied." "Then we developed the atomic bomb." "We copied all we could and just kept developing new technology in jets and other things." "The computer chip is a copy too." "Then we actually built our own "UFO" looking spacecraft." "But, we still don't have the technology right and they keep crashing." Three aliens sat inside the spacecraft and one of them operated a lever to open the dome. The aliens climbed out and made a gesture to Jake. "What's he saying?" Jake asked Bill. "I think he knows you or something." The ground began to shake and vibrate. "The spacecraft is gone!" "Damn it!" Bill yelled. "I wanted them to explain their Ion Drive and Warp Engines." "The Anti Grav Engines and lasers too." "They wouldn't tell you Bill." "We already copied the shit out of them and now they're pissed off at us." Suzie said.. Jake had some kind of a devise in his hand. "What the hell is this and where did it come from?" He shouted. I'll figure this out later." "I doubt it." Bill said. "But, let me tell you." "This could be the end of Mankind's reign on this planet Earth." "These aliens are far ahead of us in technology and could wipe us out." "The Air Force and our government don't want us to know this." "That's one of the reasons for all of the lies and cover ups of UFO sightings." "I hope the hell you're wrong." Jake said.

"Did we get all that on film Dan?" Jake asked. "Yes sir and let's get it on the CNN news tonight." They raced back to the hotel and set up for the broadcast. "This is Dan Miller reporting for CNN from the Grand Canyon." "With me are Jake Green, Suzie Green and Bill Wilson." "Bill, what is it?" Dan asked. "It's the future Dan and I'm afraid it could be the end for Mankind." "What do you mean?" "I mean that the aliens are far, far ahead of us here on Earth." "They have weapons that could wipe us all out in a matter of hours." "If they decide to use them we're finished." "Mankind's reign on Earth is ended!!" "The film and tape footage you are about to see was shot today near here in the desert." "I assure you it is genuine." Dan said to the world as the people watched in horror! They rolled the film and audio and answered questions from the call in line. Afterwards they celebrated in the hotel bar. "That should convince even the most hard core cynic." Jake said.

They all went their separate ways the next day. Jake and Suzie took off for California, but along the way were pulled over by highway patrol cops. The trooper wanted Jake's ID and took him into the cruiser. Inside the cruiser was none other then Decker. "Hi fuck face." "Remember me." "I'm the guy you bashed over the head with the shovel." "We've got a little surprise for you two." "Look Decker why don't we just forget the whole thing." "We're even now." Decker slapped Jake in the face and maced him. "What's the matter pecker breath are we crying?" Decker yelled as he and his men loaded Suzie and Jake into the white jeeps and took off. "You're on your way to do hard time for life shit for brains." "Your girlfriend is headed for the woman's slammer in Texas." "I warned you asshole and now your gona pay." Decker punched Jake in the face breaking his nose. "Take her fucking cloths off." Decker told his men. "Now throw her cloths out the window." "She won't need them where she's going." Jake had one slight chance to escape. He still had the alien devise the alien gave him. He tried to turn it on and nothing happened. "What the fuck are you doing moron?" Decker yelled. Suddenly Decker disappeared and the Jeep stopped. "I'll use this again if I have to." Jake said. He and Suzie took off in a Jeep and found their car. "Poor, pitiful Decker." Suzie said. "Yea, I guess I zapped him!" Jake said while hauling ass across the desert. "We'll be in Fairfield by midnight."

CHAPTER 10:

WHAT GOES UP IS NEVER COMING BACK DOWN

"With Decker and his cretin minions finally out of the way we can work on proving our case." "No more Air Force hassle and crap." Jake told Suzie as they sped along in the "FBI" Ford. They had been home at Jake's pad for a few days rest and were on their way to the law school. "I'm filing a legal brief demanding that the Air Force fess up on all of it." "We tried that before Jake!" "It didn't work!" "I know and I'll keep trying till my dying day." "That'll be pretty damned soon if you keep this up." They pulled into a truck stop on route 66 near the New Mexico and and Arizona border. The "Old 666 Diner", was the best place to eat on the highway. The waitress' wore skin tight shorts, were topless and had devil's horns on their heads. "I danced here once a long time ago." Suzie said with an evil grin. They found a table right in the middle of the dining room. The place was busy 24/7 and a little crazy. "What'll you have sexy?" The waitress asked Jake while she rubbed his back. "I, I . yi think I'll, I'll have ...." "What can I get that's hot?" "Whatever you want sugar." She had a huge set of size thirty sixes and kept leaning over in Jake's face. "I'll take everything." "How bout you honey?" "Same for me missy." Suzie said. Jake seemed very pleased with himself and said, "just for your info honey "everything" is a huge breakfast of steak and eggs, pancakes and orange juice."

As they were trying to finish some of their huge breakfast, two old timers came over to their table. "Mind if we join ya mister?" They smelled like cow manure and were filthy. "Go ahead old timers." Jake said. "We been haulin beef on the hoof for bout a week." "We been mining too." "Ma name is Guy Wood and this hare is Fred Ober." "We used ta be them thar social worker guys and I was in charge." "How'd ya like that thar young fella?" "You were in charge?" Jake asked with disbelief. "I can't member, I..." "Maybe Fred hare was.." "So tell me what's been going on around here?" Jake asked. "Nuthin much cept tham damn Air Force war games." Yea, they been flying tham saucers again they have." Freddy said. "It don't make no matter ta us cept that noise." "Bout ta make us deef!" Guy said as he drooled on the table."Where about was this" Jake asked. 'Huh, what's ya say young fella?" Fred asked as he spit tobacco juice in a glass. He had all black rotten teeth. "Where?" "Nar them Superstitions, that there is a ware." Guy said as he scratched his filthy hair. "I ciant member ta good na mare yas naw." Guy said. "I done drove ma car inta da back end a truck and a got me brain damage!" ""Yes sir a done it ta masalf!" 'The Superstition Mountains you say?" Jake asked. "Yea pilgrim that there is wat I said I a reckin." "Twas a mighty loud thunder that it made ya knaw." Freddy said. "Yep, I thought it'd kill us fur sewer." Guy said. "We done cleared out a thare." "We heard tell twas some miners killed up in them there Superstitions by them there Air Force thangs." "Them wus rale purdy, bright lights tho." I spect twas saucer shaped them was, them rally twas." "Okay old timers just tell us where you were."

"Man!" "They smelled like rotten garbage and cow shit mixed together!" Jake said to Suzie as they drove towards the Superstitions. "That's probably about right!" Suzie said. "I almost gagged when Fred Ober spit that gross, lunger of shitty chewing tobacco in the glass." She said. "His breath was even worse then the stinky cloths." "It smelled like dog shit or something." "I don't think anybody around here goes to the dentist or takes a bath!" Suzie said. "Yep, I a reckon far sure." Jake said laughing. It was 115 degrees in Phoenix and as they cruised along with the AC blasting she said, "maybe we'll find the Lost Dutchman Mine and the aliens!" They parked the car at a rental place for horses and packed their supplies on a pack mule. "I figure one day in to the camping area on the map." Jake said. It had gotten cooler and the wind started howling. They rode in for a few hours and had gone about ten miles when the weather got nasty. "Jake what about this sand storm?" "We'll have to hunker down baby." "They found a deserted cabin and old barn for the horses. "We may as well get a fire going and stay here." Jake said. "Do you want Denny Moore Beef Stew or Denny Moore Beef Stew?" Jake said laughing. "Why do you find that stupid question so funny?" "It really isn't is it?" He kept laughing and Suzie clobbered him in the head with a sleeping bag. "There cretin!" After dinner Suzie told Jake the place gave her the creeps. "It sure is spooky here at night." Suzie said. ""Well, it is the Superstitions!" "The lost Dutchman Mine and all kinds of other tales of wield happenings." "What was that noise outside Jake?" "Probably nothing." "Will you please go check it out?" "Okay baby", he said as he got a jacket on and went out the door. "Nothing much out here but sand and wind." Jake said to himself. "I'll check the horses and head back inside." "These Superstition Mountains are creepy." "Who knows what the hell is around here." "Hey you!" Jake saw a man with a pack mule near the barn. "Hey you wait!" He ran over to where the man was and nothing was there. "That is very strange." "I'll look around and head back inside." After about half an hour he didn't see anything and went back inside. "Suzie I thought I saw someone with a pack mule, but he disappeared." "Yea sure Jake." "No really I did." "Then why didn't you find him?" "I looked and he was gone." "Then come to bed."

She noticed the bulge in Jake's pants and said, "what's that my horny Jakster?" "Oh, that?" "Yea, that?" "Well, you never know if you might get lucky." He said. "Jump in this sleeping bag and we'll see my lover boy."

They headed out early the next day and found a huge tower like rock on top of a mountain peak. "This is "Tower Rock" according to the map." "Let's camp here tonight." Jake said. "By the way lover, "Tower Rock" is haunted." Jake said laughing. "Thar been some mighty strange thangs goin on I reckon." Jake said laughing while Suzie tried to ignore him. "Me Tarzan, you Jane UG!" Now she really couldn't ignore him and threw some dirt at him. "Hey, wait a second, there's gold in this rock!" "It's the Lost Dutchman Mine!" Jake said. Suzie came running over to him. "Where, where is it!" "Right here." "It's fools gold!" "Alright you creep you are in for it now buster!"

Later, after they ate the last of the Denny Moore Beef Stew, some strange lights appeared in the sky, but seemed to stay in one place all night. "They appear to be rotating or spinning around." Jake said as he looked through his binoculars. "Why aren't they coming any nearer to us?" Suzie asked. "It must be an Apache chopper on silent mode." Jake said. "You can't hear them in silent mode," The lights made no movement or noise. The next night the same lights appeared in the same place. "It looks the same to me." Jake said while looking through his binoculars. "It's the damned Apaches again." Suddenly the light began to move rapidly in all directions. "They're doing 90 degree turns in space." "That is impossible for our aircraft." Jake said. "Unless, the Air Force has developed something new." Suzie said as they watched the lights vanish from the sky. "That was amazing!" They both said. "Do you think the lights were launched from Earth." "I don't know Suzie." "But, if they were they're never coming back!"

After wandering around in the mountains for a few more days and getting really thirsty, they packed it in. "I'm ready for some really ice cold cans of Bud baby." "That sounds really good Jake." They made it back later that day and returned to the 666 Diner. I think they're using this mountain range for testing some of their high tech stuff." Jake said while they had ice cold beers and burgers."That is for sure mister." A voice said from behind Jake. "Mind if I sit a spell?" "Sure go ahead." Jake said. "I'm Billy Lizard Jr." "I overheard you talking about the lights in the sky." "I can assure you they are man made." "The Air Force is testing new drones or unmanned aircraft over there." "The area around the Superstitions is isolated and good for the testing in secret." "There's a few prospectors up their, but that's about all." "They keep the tourists away from the area where the testing takes place." "Is there a prospector up there near an old cabin?" Jake asked. "Yea, you must have seen the "Old Gold Miner." "Some say he's a ghost and some say he's real." Billy said. "Well, I saw him." Jake said. "Then you may have seen a ghost!" Billy said laughing. "So, what about these drones?" Jake asked. "Once they launch they never come back down to Earth." "Where do they go?" Suzie asked Billy. "They fly around spying on people and places and take pictures, then electronically send the pictures back to Air Force headquarters." "They self destruct after awhile or when they go below 5000 feet." "That way no one can locate them and the Air Force keeps their secrets." "That is amazing." Jake said. "How do you know about this sir?" Suzie asked. "Simple." "I invented them." "They fired me one year ago after I protested about the pollution and littering they are causing." "Now I'm out of a job." " I'm Unemployed!" "Not anymore sir." Jake said. "How would you like to work for me and CNN?" "I'd love to!" "You're hired!" "Tell us more about these Air Force drones." Jake said to Billy.

After three more days on the road they made it to the law school. Billy met them and began his research for Jake. "You know Billy those drones you invented are like the military brass and bureaucrats running our government." "They take off on their "Careers", fly around ruining people's lives and then self destruct." "They are mindless and have no ethical standards or moral beliefs." "They're freaking drones!" "I kind of like the "Unmanned Drone Concept", because it represents our military and governmental leaders in this country." "Yea, I know." Billy said. "I thought of that when I first started developing them." "But, it was too late." "The military loved them and put them in use immediately!" "Let's take them and the bureaucratic assholes down!" Jake said. "That's a deal Jake."

Jake wrote his legal brief and filed it with the federal Court in Burlington. It took six months for the case to finally be heard by the court. Jake's main argument was that the obvious cover ups deprived the American people of the knowing the truth about UFOs. "Major Armstrong do you feel that the American people deserve to know the truth about UFOs?" "Yes I do." "Then why don't you tell the court all about it here and now." Jake asked. "You mean disobey my orders?" "Yes sir I do." "Well, I just can't do that Green." "Major Armstrong is this the Air Force' version of the "Don't ask, Don't Tell Policy?" The court erupted with laughter. "I have no further comment Attorney Green!" "Major tell the court about the nuclear waste contamination at the Yucca Mountain Waste Facility." "The what?" "You heard me sir." "Isn't it true that over 45 transports of the nuclear waste have either leaked or were spilled contaminating the area where the trucks were?" "I have no idea Green." The Major answered. "Your honor please advised the witness that he is in contempt of court for refusing to answer the question put to him." "Well major what do you have to say?" Judge Mahady said. "I have no further comment." "Sheriff take Major Armstrong to the PD for processing and lock him up for contempt of court." The judge ordered. " This Court is in recess."

The next day the story appeared in the Times and most other newspapers. The Air Force brass were out for Jake's head! The Times article read: "Air Force Brass wage all out war on Attorney

Green." "Green to testify before Congress." Six months later in congress Jake testified. "Mr. Green do you actually expect us to believe that UFOs exist and that you have seen them and that our nation is polluting the country side with nuclear waste?" Senator Lackey asked. "No sir I don't expect you to believe anything that the Air Force has instructed you not to believe." Jake said as the floor of the U.S. Congress erupted in laughter. "Sir your insubordination exceeds even your high degree of ignorance by a country mile!" "Now, kindly answer my question sir!" "Senator, I have seen UFOs shot down by the Air Force." "Go on Mr. Green you're hanging yourself pretty well all by yourself." The Senator said. "I have seen all these things and will prove it." "Just how do you plan to do that?" "By showing you and the entire Senate and all of the world my films!" Suzie then wheeled a projector into the Senate and played the film. It lasted two full hours and showed all the polluted areas and the captured alien bodies. The Senators were ready to recess for the day when Jake shocked them." "This my friends and honorable Senators is the devise the alien gave me." Jake held the alien devise up showing everyone. He fired it at a statue of Lyndon Johnson and it disappeared. "Any questions?" "Yes sir I have one." The vice president said. "How long do you plan to leave Major Armstrong locked up in prison Mr. Green?" "As long as it takes to get the truth from him and the Air Force." "Until he and the USAF tell the whole truth about UFOs and the nuclear waste pollution." The next day the Times story said, "attorney Green performs magic show in U.S. Senate." "Senators irate at the waste of taxpayers time and money!"

Chapter 11:

The Awakening

Jake was busy making a beef stew and watching CNN on the tube. "What's that smell?" "Damn!" "It's the stew!" He raced to the kitchen from the living room and saw the mess. The stew was all burnt and stuck to the pan. Smoke was filling the kitchen and setting off the smoke alarms. "Damn it what a mess!" "Good going Green!" "You sure can Cook!" "Guess I'll have hot dogs and beans." "You asshole you......."

"Wake up Jake!" "Wake up you Rip Van Winkle." "What, wha time is it?" "It's 2pm and you've been asleep for two days." "Suzie what are you doing here?" "I got here last night, don't you remember?" "I showed up with my suitcase and we made love and..." "Oh yea." "Is the story on CNN?" "What story?" "You know the UFOs." "What UFOs Jake?" "Will you get it together!" Jake jumped out of bed and was freaking out. "The desert and the UFO and CNN and..." "Jake I don't know what your talking about," "You've been right here all weekend reading sci fi books about reverse engineering of alien spacecraft." "You're a science fiction nut!" "Before that you were driving around in San Francisco and the desert looking for the damned things." "That was all last week." She said "No way!" Jake screamed. "I was with you investigating UFOs in Canada and Alaska." "Sorry dreamer boy, but that's not true." "We went to Canada and Alaska and Vermont and I passed the bar exam and became a lawyer." What!" She asked. "CNN and Decker and Air Force jets shooting down UFOs." "Jake get a grip will you!" "Suzie I was really in all those places!" "I sure as hell wasn't!" Suzie screamed. "You mean this whole thing has been a big, long dream???" "Yep it sure has!" Jake began throwing his cloths in the suitcase and packing up to leave. "Where are you going Jake?" "We're going on a trip to investigate UFOs." "I have finally found myself and it was in a dream!!!" "But, who cares because I'm a new man now baby!" "I learned that being yourself is really the only way you can live." "The old Jake Green is dead and may he rest in peace!!"

Suzie decided to humor Jake and go with him. They loaded the VW Van up with supplies and headed down the coast to the Mojave Desert and route 66. "It looks the same to me Jake." "We've been out here a shit load of times and it always looks the same." Jake was so into his driving and concentrating on proving that it wasn't all just a dream that he didn't even hear her. "Jake are you listening to me at all!" "What the hell is wrong with you?" "Sorry baby, but I'm concentrating." "No shit, I can see the smoke coming out of your ears!" As they approached Needles Jake said, "there at the body shop." "That's where I had the van painted." "Yea, that's right the van is white now and it used to be green!" "That proves I'm right!" "No it does not." "You could have had it painted any time." "Okay." "What about Dan Wilson of CNN?" "Will you believe him?" "Who's Dan Miller?" "Jake, I've never heard of him." "Do you mean Arthur Kent, the "Scud Stud?" "No, not him." "What about the UFO expert Bill Wilson?" "No, you mean Bob Lezar." No, I mean Bill Wilson!" "Okay, okay I give up, for now." As they drove along through the desert Suzie got that old deja vu again. "Jake I think I've been out here recently or something." "Yea I know you were kidnapped and tortured." "What!" "You had a dream that I was tortured!?" "You pervert!" "Are you a sadist now or something?" She asked him screaming at the top of her lungs. "No baby of course not." He said. "I mean that I feel like I've been here before ." Suzie said in a fog. "That is deja vu baby." "Look, let's go over to the Air Force Base at Victorville." "That's where we were." "Okay Jake lead on." When they arrived at the fence near George AFB Jake said, "we camped right here and saw the UFO in that hanger over there and you drove the "FBI" Ford over there to investigate." "I remember a black place and water pouring into my mouth." Suzie said. "Jake do you think we could both have had the same dream?" "It's possible baby." "Jakester, I think I love your old hippie ass." She said with her arm around him. "Don't let that go to your big, fat head!" "I love you too baby." "Let's get a room lover." "I need a good hot bath." Suzie said as she kissed Jake. They drove to Nevada near Area 51 and then checked into the "Little A'le' Inn in Rachel, Nevada. "This was worth the drive baby." "If you say so." Suzie yelled from the "Alien Tub." It was the shape of a flying saucer and had green bubbles in the water.

That night on CNN they watched the evening report. "This is Dan Miller reporting for CNN from the crash site of a UFO here in Canada's Yukon Territory." "I have UFO expert Bill Wilson with me." "Bill what is it?" "It appears to be an alien spacecraft Dan." "It has more advanced technology then our aircraft and weapons." "This could be the end for Mankind Dan." "Our reign on this planet could be over." "Why is that Bill?" Dan asked. "Maybe it's the nuclear bombs and nuclear fallout we've created." "The thousands of nuclear bombs we've detonated during "Tests" while trying to blow our beautiful planet all to hell." "The nuclear waste from reactors and nuclear weapons polluting our fresh water and our air all over the world." "The unsafe nuclear storage facilities like at Yucca Mountain Storage Facility." "The Russians dumping haw nuclear waste into rivers and the ocean." "The unstable third world countries that have nuclear weapons pointed at us and ready to fire." "The selfish, greedy humans always taking from nature and never giving back." "The depletion of our natural resources and fossil fuels by humans and their ever increasing need for more energy." "The aliens may want to wipe us out to prevent further damage to their universe from all the pollution that Mankind has spread." "Wow!" "You heard it first on CNN." Dan yelled into the microphone. "There!" "Did you hear that!" Jake yelled to Suzie. "Yea, but I don't quite believe it." "Jake could you rub my sore back?" "Sure honey." "Hey there's a scar on your shoulder honey." "How'd that get there?" "It's from the electric shocks they gave me." "Wow!" "I can't believe I said that!" "Then you remember?" "How can I ever forget it." "Now I remember those bastards torturing me with water and electric shocks." "I hope they all rot in hell!" "Oh, don't worry baby they will." "Suzie did you see this newspaper?" "There's a story about an Air Force Sergeant who was found dead in the desert." "His name was Decker!"

"You know what baby?" "We're like those UFOs that came crashing down on Earth." "Some people are either shot down or just self destruct and crash here on our planet." Jake said while Suzie listened intently. "They are unidentified people who have no real life on Earth flying around in a meaningless existence, just mere objects in a world they are trying to destroy. "The world is full of people like that." "That's right Jake." She said. "They're like UFOs." "I know people who have just crashed into the ground, so to speak." "Now they're either dead or lifeless, walking dead." "Especially all the military leaders and scientists who have contributed to the Nuclear Weapons Race." Nuclear weapons developed for the sole purpose of destroying our planet Earth." Suzie said. "And the nuclear power plants and submarines producing nuclear waste that Mankind has no way to ever get hid of." "It's the worst kind of pollution and very deadly." Jake said. "All of those people are crashing down in flames right now as we speak!" Suzie said. "Earth is a beautiful planet and I love it." Jake said. "The splendid green fields and beautiful forests with tall, proud trees and all the wonderful and unique animals." Suzie said. "The beautiful blue sea , fresh, cold drinking water and fresh, crisp air to breath." Jake said. "Let's both pledge to do all we can to stop the world wide pollution of our planet." "You're on girl." Jake said. "Thank God we're alive Jakester." Suzie said while kissing Jake. "Suzie, this could be the end of Mankind on Earth." "It was a lonely old place wasn't it Jake?" "Yea baby until I found you." "Jake listen." "It really doesn't matter if our dreams are real or not honey." "We have found each other and know who we really are." That's what really counts in the short time that we have here on the planet Earth." "Yea, baby you're right on." Jake said as he played with an alien looking device he had in his pocket.

THE END

Sources

UFO EVIDENCE.ORG

ROSWELL UFO INCIDENT@WIKIPEDIA.ORG

AIR FORCE BASES @GLOBALSECURITY.ORG

1941 CAPE GIRARDEAU, MISSOURI CRASH@
UFOS.ABOUT.COM

MACKENZIE BAY@WIKIPEDIA

HERSCHEL ISLAND@ WIKIPEDIA

WHITE SANDS MISSILE RANGE@ WIKIPEDIA

YUCCA MOUNTAIN NUCLEAR WASTE
REPOSITORY@ WIKIPEDIA

LIST OF ALLEGED UFO CRASHES@
WIKIPEDIA

Made in the USA